Arcane Sunflower

COURTNEY SUMMERLIN

ISBN: 1449585930
ISBN-13: 9781449585938

I would like to say thank you to everyone who believed this would one day be in print. I would also like to give a big thanks to my editor Jessica Walser for the countless reads and re-reads, the emails of brainstorming, and for being a great sounding board. Without your expertise this book wouldn't be what it is today. Finally, I would like to thank my husband for standing behind me and giving me the encouragement I needed.

Contents

Chapter 1: The Library

~

I listened to the quiet whir of warm air pouring through the vents. Besides the scratch of my pencil and the faint crinkle of paper when I impatiently turned another page, everything else was still, silent. My head rested in one hand while the other fed me the end of my already half-chewed eraser. I looked up from the long wooden table, scattered with books and carefully strewn notebook paper. To the average person it probably looked like an utter mess, but I had a specific place for each scrap.

I'm pretty smart, no genius of course, but I'd made it through the first few weeks of college without a hitch. I was glad to be in the middle of the semester even though midterms were looming and even though I still had no idea what I wanted to major in. I was no longer lumped in to the "fresh meat" category. I was past the stage of having my face tucked into a map in between classes and I'd thankfully dodged the legendary "I'll sell you an elevator pass, they're only for seniors," prank. There wasn't a single elevator to be found on campus. Apparently, when the university was built, whoever made the decisions was bent on making sure the students had their share of exercise between classes. As if walking the small city-sized campus wasn't enough.

I sank into a daze as I stared at the high walls packed neatly from end to end with books and the thick wooden bookshelves that stood in perfect lines to create tight little aisles. All were cataloged and organized precisely. I should know since I worked for the library part time. Truth be told, the library had become a sort of second home, a world of literature that I knew inside and out packed into five floors. I liked the fifth floor. Students rarely came here because it was full of nothing but periodicals and old poetry books. Peace and quiet, my favorite.

I had a reason to be here so late, her name was Erin and she was my roommate. I sighed, wondering how her party was going. I'd escaped shortly after seven knowing she'd inevitably try to drag me into her night of hapless fun. I never would've been able to study—correction cram—with all the noise and booming music. With that thought, my eyes wandered down to the book in front of me full of lines and numbers I'd spent the last few hours trying to understand. I hated trigonometry. I groaned, realizing I still hadn't studied for history or literature. The two books perched harmlessly on the farthest edge of the table. I breathed in, trying to revive myself before scowling at the clear plastic Starbuck's cup that stood empty with a ring of water forming around its base. If only I'd listened to the little metal box at the drive thru and ordered a grande instead of a measly medium. I looked back down at my book, forcing my mind to work just a little longer.

When I finally glanced up at the small clock above the stairwell door it was near midnight. I yawned, letting my pencil slip from my stiff fingers as I wiggled them to get the blood flowing again. I sat there debating how much longer I wanted to postpone the cold walk back to my jeep when I noticed movement out of the corner of my eye. A heavy rush of air swirled behind me before two icy hands grabbed my shoulders. I took a deep breath to let out a scream but only silence passed through my lips.

My eyes snapped open to a landscape of rolling hills of books and paper, my pencil leaning sloppily in my hand. I must've fallen asleep. The stairwell door caught my attention as it was slowly closing. I lifted my head, looking to see who had come in. My heart was still pounding in my chest. *It was only a dream*, I told myself over and over again, trying to convince the small whisper in my head that believed the dream was about to become reality. There was a shadow of movement to my right. My head reflexively turned to see him standing in one of the narrow aisles, staring at me.

I quickly looked down to hide the sudden red in my cheeks. He was tall, with creamy, ivory colored skin and dark eyes that peered out from a distinct, but gentle and almost boyish looking face. His satin, deep brown hair was rumpled with a few strands that swept across his forehead that was creased into a frown. He was gorgeous. I could feel the weight of his stare, but couldn't stop myself from peaking out of the corner of my eye as I tucked my hair behind one ear. He was gone. I leaned back in the chair, its wooden body creaking in protest as I looked around only to find the library to be the quiet emptiness it always was. I've got to quit reading all those vampire novels, I thought. I pinched my arm as hard as I could to make completely sure I was fully conscious. Yep, it hurt. I must be awake. Apparently, fatigue and my imagination had gotten the best of me, so I decided to stop the studying for the evening. I could hear my fluffy covers and warm cotton sheets calling to me.

As I was neatly shoving my books into my ragged canvas pack I found myself wondering if maybe he had been real, maybe it wasn't just my overactive mind that had been overworked with countless hours of math. Even so, I couldn't get past the expression on his face. It was like he had some unmet curiosity. The two dark lines above his eyes had been pulled together and his lips had been pressed into a tight line. He had looked like a Greek statue, minus the blank look and replaced with a frustrated frown. I didn't recognize him. Hard as I tried I couldn't figure out why he'd stood there so long, staring.

He must have been thinking about whether or not to talk to me I decided. It figured that he opted to walk away after coming to the conclusion that I wasn't approachable material, just like everyone else. I'm not unattractive, but I'm also not the blonde, perfect body cheerleader type. I'm petite with long, copper colored hair and blonde highlights, bright green eyes, and a fair complexion. I stand out in my own way. My dad always said my eyes could be seen from miles away because they were the color of the trees with morning dew. When I was little he'd say, "When the sun hits each leaf at the perfect spot they throw shiny glints of light that pierce the forest floor, that's the color of your eyes Ansley." The memory made my chest ache.

I missed them. Although, when I graduated and was pushed into going to college, I was happy to get out of Salem. I enjoyed the smaller town of Corvallis and treated it as a fresh start, leaving high school and its uncomfortable awkwardness behind.

I opened the door to the outside world and shivered as the cool night air rushed past me. It was going to be a long walk back to my jeep. I took in a deep breath of the crisp air and began treading down the long concrete steps then headed left on the paved walk towards the parking lot. The university prided itself on its "woodsy" feel with its countless patches of trees and bushes. Everywhere you looked there was some sort of foliage. Sometimes it felt like the middle of nowhere instead of a college campus. Thankfully, it was well lit so I didn't have to carry a flashlight or worry about all the shadowed places along the path. Even with all the dense wood-like feeling, it felt safe.

I noticed suddenly that tonight felt different. I was getting a strange vibe that I was being watched. It was that itch between my shoulder blades, the reason my hair stood on end. I did a quick look back in mid stride and an even quicker glance around to the few places the fluorescent lights failed to touch. There was only the faint hum of the lamps and the quiet beat of my tennis shoes against the pavement. Everything was still; quiet, as if the night was holding its breath waiting for something to happen. I had slowly started to quicken my pace, trying as hard as I could to pretend I wasn't spooked when I heard a faint whisper behind me, as if someone were letting out a frustrated sigh. I froze. My heart was trying to beat itself out of my chest while my brain was screaming run to my legs that wouldn't budge. I slowly turned my head in the direction of the sound. Nothing. I looked around again, my eyes darting back and forth, scanning my surroundings. Nothing. I stood there a few more seconds waiting for something to jump out at me while I calmed my breathing. I let out a sigh.

"Geez Ansley, get a grip," I huffed to myself as I shuffled my feet back into motion.

The door to my old red jeep groaned as I opened it to toss my pack in the passenger's seat. I pulled myself in before simultaneously sticking the key in the ignition and pressing the clutch down. My left leg stretched to hold it in place as I turned the key. The engine stuttered a few times before it roared to life and finally idled at a low rumble. I loved my jeep. It was rusted and old, but it had gotten me through high school. Meaning, it had saved me from riding a school bus full of boys who stared and girls who shunned and avoided me. I'd had to deal with the awkwardness enough just by walking through the halls. I remember how I'd so often felt like I had an invisible bubble around me. If they were walking in a group together the other students would always part in the middle so they could walk a wide circle around me, huddling back again once they'd passed me. The boys always stopped to gawk, their eyes wide with what seemed to be fear while the girls glared and whispered amongst themselves. I hadn't needed any more than that.

I pulled the knob out for the heater and clicked on the lights before revving the engine slightly to ease out of the parking lot. The radio had been rendered incapacitated long before I'd had the vehicle, so I listened to the even rumble of the engine as I headed home.

The brakes announced my arrival, squeaking as I slowed to a stop on the edge of the sidewalk in front of a small two story house that was still surrounded by a few cars. I sighed. Apparently Erin's party wasn't over yet. I sat there a moment weighing how badly I wanted to sleep in my warm bed. I could just crawl in the back of the jeep. Sure, I'd wake up feeling like a human pretzel, but at least I would avoid the stares of the party goers.

I thought back to the first time I pulled up to this house. I'd sat there staring longingly, much like I was now, at its antique trimmings and wooden porch with a white bench swing hanging on one side. It was better than I'd imagined after listening to a chipper, high keening voice describe it to me on the phone days before as I packed to move down. I remember worrying that she'd turn out to be like all the other girls I'd ever met in my life, that she'd look at me then give me some reason it wasn't going to work and slam the door in my face. I'd shuffled up the thin brick walk and held my breath as I pushed the small round doorbell. A tall and lean girl with short curly golden blonde hair and sparkling blue eyes had answered the door. I'd mustered up a weak smile,

"Hi, I'm Ansley, we…" The breath I'd been holding whooshed out as she flung her arms around me in a hug.

"I'm so excited you're here!" she'd laughed, leaning away as I stood there in utter shock.

"You're going to love it here!" she had added cheerfully.

From that point on we were inseparable, although in some ways we were complete opposites. She was scatterbrained; I took time to consider all possible options. She was a socialite; I could usually be found lost in one of my many books.

I sighed as I grabbed my bag and slid out of the jeep. I trudged up the walk, pausing before I turned the cold metal knob to open the door. I quickly mapped out the house in my head—about five steps to the stairs, then down the short hall and then finally the safety of my room. Nodding to myself in agreement, I pushed open the wooden door and slid my jacket off in short quick movements as I closed the door behind me. With my coat hung on the wall I turned towards my first checkpoint, the stairs, not daring to glance around me. I took them two at a time, not stopping as I reached my second checkpoint, the hall. Finishing the few paces to my room, I quickly shut the door behind me, glad to have gotten to my destination without being discovered.

I could feel the long night of studying weighing me down. I kicked off my shoes, pulled on my sweats and faded Slipknot shirt, and slid under the sheets of my welcoming bed. I felt a sudden plop as a large ball of fur landed on the cloud of covers. Webster, Erin's solid black cat, padded his way through the mounds of fabric towards my head.

"How did you get in here?" I asked. I scratched him on the head while he proceeded to curl himself into a tight circle on my pillow. With his soft purring as a lullaby, I took a deep breath and drifted to sleep.

I tossed and turned the next morning trying to decide how badly I wanted to get up. I still had a heap of studying waiting for me that I wasn't so eager to dive into.

Erin made the decision for me with a light knock on my door.

I groaned as she opened the door slowly. "Weren't you up late last night too? Why aren't you trying to catch up on sleep like I'm currently trying to do?"

She smiled at me as she glided over to my bed with her laptop in hand.

"I do have to study some time. You know my parents won't let me keep this place if I lose my scholarship," she reminded me as she eased onto the end of my bed. Erin's parents were extremely well off and paid for practically everything she wanted, which worked out well for me because it meant my rent was almost nothing.

I nodded as she pulled open her laptop. We listened to the familiar clicks and groans as it slowly came to life.

"So, what'cha got planned for the day?" she said absently as she clicked the little buttons.

I sighed, rubbing my eyes. "Studying, of course."

She smiled. "You missed out on a good party."

"Bummer," I said in between a yawn before adding, "what're you doing today? Or were you serious, you're actually going to do a little book work?"

Her smile grew wider, "Thanks for the sarcasm. Scott invited me out to his family's estate for the weekend. He wants us to have dinner with his parents tonight."

"Which guy is this again, I get so confused?"

"Ha, ha. Ya know, if you weren't always reading or working at the library and took a look around, you might have noticed that a good majority of the guys here are constantly checking you out."

I snorted. "There are more interesting things to life than the way Scott's, wait no...Jake's...I mean Matt's, I've lost track of them all, pants fit around their butts." She threw a pillow at me.

"At least I *have* a boyfriend."

I nodded. "A few."

She shrugged. "I like to keep my options open. About you though, Shawn is definitely interested."

I rolled my eyes. "I bet he is with all of his gawking and wide-eyed staring, with our total lack of conversation. He doesn't even know me."

"Seriously though Ansley, if you just give him a chance; he's probably just nervous."

"I don't know…we'll see." *Nervous,* sure like every other guy has been in my life. I'm a freak somehow. Everyone else seems to see it but Erin.

I tried to change the topic. "Since we're talking about guys, I saw someone interesting last night." She clicked her laptop shut and clasped her fingers together on top it, flashing her expectant eyes at me like she always does when she's truly interested in something. I hesitated, regretting the topic.

"Who, where, tell me, was he hot?" She shifted restlessly when I didn't automatically gush with details, eagerly waiting for my response.

I blew out and in a rush let the words mush together, "I don't know who, in the library of course, he was… very nice." The words sounded funny coming from me, but my lips thinned into a smile nonetheless.

She gasped, "You're blushing!"

I threw the covers off and stood, searching for a way to hide my face. Rummaging through my closet seemed to be good enough as any.

"What else? What'd he look like? What'd you talk about?" She was practically bouncing on the edge of my bed.

I sighed. I could see there was no way to avoid this. She'd nag me until I broke and gave up any and all information. So, I turned back around and plopped down next to her.

"I don't know. He was tall, had dark hair, a little pale, I guess." *Completely gorgeous.* I couldn't admit that to her though, I'd never hear the end of it.

"We didn't talk. It was weird, I looked up and he was there, staring at me. I looked away for a second and when I looked back again, he was gone. The strangest part was his eyes and the *way* he was looking at me. Like he was waiting for something to happen."

She frowned, "Hmm, that is kinda odd. Maybe he thought you were hot."

My mind wandered to the question of why he'd been at the library so late on a Friday night, especially on the floor that students rarely went to. Maybe he needed to do research for a project? No, there shouldn't have been anyone else there; no one goes that late—besides me, of course. It just didn't make sense.

"Did you know a Rachel Thoma?" Erin's question brought me back to the conversation. She had re-opened her laptop and was looking through the daily college news, something she did every morning.

I blinked, running the name through my head. "No, why?"

"Says here she was found dead outside the arts building early this morning," she said, her voice quavering slightly.

I froze. The library was right next to the arts building.

"Holy crows, how creepy is that? Did you see anybody when you left last night?"

"No, what else does it say?" I slid backwards on my bed so that I could lean against the wall to look over Erin's shoulder. A picture of a young girl stood out against the thick black letters that read:

"COLLEGE STUDENT FOUND MAULED"

"Just says some lawn maintenance guy found her behind some bushes early this morning. Says it looks like an animal attack of some sort. Her body was sent for autopsy but no word on what the cause of death was. They interviewed her roommate who said that Rachel had spent the last few weeks in the arts building working on a project that she was trying to finish for the upcoming art show.

The Dean is asking anyone who might have been in the area last night or this morning to come by the administrator's office and put forth any information possible. He is also warning all students to travel in groups for a while until they figure out who or what did this," she finished reading, her excited mood now dissolved.

We both sat silently for a minute. I started thinking about my walk last night and shuddered.

Erin looked at me eyes wide, "What if that guy you saw…" She stopped mid sentence, slowly shaking her head.

"Nah, just a weird coincidence, I was beat. I probably just imagined him or something. You know how I get." She smiled, but the words were already out and I couldn't help another involuntary shudder. How had he gotten in last night? I was sure I'd locked the door behind me.

She shrugged. "Guess you have something to do to put off studying for a little while."

I stood, arms over head, fingers reaching in one of those full on morning stretches.

"Guess so." I said, deflated.

Truth was I would have rather studied. I was always one of those quiet types that could usually be found curled up with my head stuck in a book whose creased cover had definitely seen better days. I wasn't looking forward to being interrogated. Why didn't I just stay here to study yesterday?

I decided the best thing to do was prolong the inevitable by taking a much needed shower. I headed down the hall to one of the two small bathrooms. I let the hot water relax my tense muscles as I lathered my coconut scented shampoo into my hair. When my fingers began to look like prunes and the bathroom smelled like a Hawaiian getaway, I figured it was probably time to get out. I toweled off and began brushing my teeth, meanwhile trying to figure out exactly what I was going to say. *Hi, I was at the library last night. Saw some creepy guy, but I'm not sure if I really saw him or if I was just exhausted. Felt like I was being followed on my way back to my jeep. By the way, I'm not crazy or anything.* With my luck, they'd want to take me to be evaluated to see if I was really was nuts.

I figured I might as well look halfway decent so I dried my hair and slapped on some concealer and blush. I quickly chose a pair of jeans and long sleeved shirt from my closet.

"Hey how cold is it supposed to be today?" I asked loud enough so she could hear me from the other room.

"Cold and rainy," she yelled back. She was always right about the weather, it was uncanny. After slipping on my tennis shoes I grabbed my OSU sweatshirt. I took a quick look in the mirror, making sure everything looked in place, scratched Webster on the head, stuck my wallet in my back pocket, and headed downstairs.

I walked down the brick path admiring the gloomy morning. Everything around me seemed to quietly hint that it was October, from the burnt orange and deep red leaf-filled trees, to the heavy rolling dark clouds. I tossed my bag in the seat next to me and turned the key. The rust bucket always had trouble starting when it was cold, but it eventually turned over with a loud guttural rumble. I shifted to first and headed down the quiet street toward school.

There was a different energy on campus today. I could feel the tense atmosphere when I opened the door to the administrator's office. Although the room looked much like any other office with a high counter facing the entrance, a few desks behind it stacked with papers, filing cabinets lining the walls, and a large door to the right with bold letters printed "DEAN", the fear and worry radiating from it's occupants was so dense it felt like it was sticking to my skin, weighing me down. The sun was even blotted out by dark rain clouds so that no light passed through the large windows to brighten the bland office walls.

I pulled the door closed behind me and walked to the counter. A woman who looked to be in her late forties with short, chin length, mouse brown hair, dressed in what can only be described as typical school official garb—a muted green blouse and black slacks— glanced up over her glasses from one the paper ridden desks.

"Can I help you?" She looked back down, shuffling papers and placing them neatly together to staple. There were two other women in the room about the same age standing next to the filing cabinets speaking in a hushed tone. I stood there for a second trying to figure out exactly what I was going to say. I'd already rehearsed it a few times in my mind, but now, when the time had come I couldn't seem to get the words out.

She looked up again, this time really looking at me.

"What can I do for you?"

I had to say something, so I let it out in a rush.

"I saw the thing in the paper about the murder and I came to talk to someone because I was at the library last night and I'm not sure if I can really help but I figured I still should come down here because it asked for anyone who was there to stop by." I took a deep breath, glad I had managed to get everything out without stammering like an idiot.

The two women by the filing cabinets had stopped talking and were looking at me with equally troubled faces. The woman behind the desk pulled off her glasses, letting them dangle on the chord around her neck while she stood and walked over to the counter.

"Your name?" she asked as she grabbed a pad of yellow sticky paper and a pen.

I tucked a loose strand of hair behind my ear, something I do when I'm nervous.

"Ansley Welsh Ma'am." I watched as she loosely scribbled my name across the square of paper. She separated the piece from the pad and placed the stack back behind the counter.

"Have a seat and I'll let the Dean know that you're here." She turned and headed toward the heavy wooden door. After two light knocks she opened it and slipped through, clicking it shut behind her. I turned toward the few chairs that lined the wall in front of the counter and flopped down. The two women in the corner had already continued their muted conversation, their words now streaming in hurried whispers. I tried to tune out what they were saying because I really didn't want to know anything else that would make me wonder about last night. Inevitably, I still managed to hear a few pieces of unwanted information.

"They're saying it happened some time around midnight."

The shorter, slightly pudgy women let her mouth drop open in surprise. "Do you really think it was an animal?" She stuck a few pieces of paper into a folder and proceeded to thumb through the others to find its place. Meanwhile, the taller of the two squinted over the folder in her hands as she mulled over the question.

"I don't know, no. I mean, what animals do we have around here that could do that amount of damage?"

The shorter one slid the folder into its spot and was pulling out another. "Coyotes? But they wouldn't do that much damage. Besides they're skittish." The taller of the two nodded in agreement.

The door to my right opened as the first woman stepped out motioning to me.

"He's ready for you," she said, eyeing me as I stood and smiled meekly. I stepped past her and the door labeled "DEAN". I listened to it click shut behind me as I stood there waiting.

It was how I had always guessed a college Dean's office would look. The walls were lined with cherry stained wooden shelves that were full of thick books crushed together in a straight and orderly fashion. A number of plaques and framed certificates decorated a small area of wall space that wasn't trodden with books. The room reminded me of a library with the faint smell of aged paper and heavy silence. The only noise was the soft click of the large clock perched on the fire mantel that was centered on the wall behind the focal point of the room, a large desk, the same deep color as the wood on the walls. Two leather chairs sat kitty-corner in front of it. The heavy brass name plate on the desk read, "Dr. Reilly Blake". When I finally looked at the person sitting behind the desk I was surprised to find that the man in the seat didn't look like a Dean. He wasn't old with gray, translucent wrinkly skin but looked rather young, much like a runway model instead of an upper level school executive. He had short, sandy colored hair and when he looked up from his papers I noticed his dark blue eyes and fair complexion. He smiled as he gestured toward one of the chairs.

"Ansley, please have a seat." I slowly took the few steps over to one of the large leather chairs and slid down across from the man labeled Dr. Reilly Blake.

"So, I hear that you were at the library last night?" He looked back down at his papers, scribbling something before looking back at me.

I tucked my hair behind my ear and nodded. "Around eleven." His eyebrows came together as he scribbled another line.

He glanced up at me again. "Did you notice anything odd while you were there or when you were leaving?"

I let out a sigh trying to decide whether or not I should tell him about the guy I thought I saw. He silently waited, his eyes analyzing as if he were memorizing my every move and expression.

"I was on the fifth floor studying and thought I might have seen a guy in one of the aisles. He was tall with dark hair." Dr. Blake scribbled a few more lines.

"What was he wearing? Did he say anything to you?" I thought about this for a minute because the main thing I had noticed was his eyes. I didn't want to admit to it because I thought it sounded kind of silly. It took me a few seconds to recall what he'd actually been wearing.

"I think he had on blue jeans and a dark shirt, but I'm not completely sure. It was late and I was pretty tired from studying and no he didn't say anything to me."

He smiled again, "Ah yes, midterms are here aren't they." He went back to writing again. "Do you remember anything else?"

I shook my head, "No, not really." He nodded while continuing to write.

"Alright then, I'm going to relay this information to the detective. He may stop by your home later on today, so be prepared to repeat what you've passed on to me and try to remember anything else you can between now and then."

I nodded and got up to leave. He watched me carefully, a sort of curiosity in his eyes while he added, "Thank you for stopping by Ansley. Please be careful around campus for the next few weeks until we figure out what's going on."

I nodded again. "Yes, sir."

I opened the door and walked back into the waiting area with my head down, eyes focusing on the plain office carpet. An odd tingling swept across my skin. When I looked up *he* was standing there. I froze, my heart sputtered and raced as my eyes recognized the tall form dressed in khaki pants and a dark polo shirt standing at the counter talking with the woman who had helped me. I couldn't believe what I was seeing. He was real. I could see now, in the well lit room that he wasn't as slight as I'd thought. His skin hinted at lean, hard muscles that stretched beneath the smooth surface.

It sounded like they were discussing his schedule, but I wasn't entirely certain, having walked in on the middle of the conversation. She was smiling up at him, her features animated as she spoke, while he stood there mirroring her expression. She sure seemed a lot happier talking to him than she did me. Well he *was* stunning. His voice, although muted, was a perfect mixture of smooth and rough; the sound made my cheeks burn. When she looked down to type into the computer he turned his head in my direction and his eyes locked on mine as his face formed the same curious interest as last night. He looked as if he were frustrated and waiting for something that still hadn't happened. I stared into the dark pools of his eyes. The hair on my arms stood as my palms started to sweat. I didn't know whether to turn around and go back into Dr. Blake's office or dart for the door and sprint back to my jeep to speed home and hide under my covers. Something was telling me I was in danger, but I couldn't make myself move. The air started to sweep in and out of my lungs as I unsuccessfully tried to keep my breathing normal. I couldn't look away from his dark gaze. It was as if his eyes were trying to tell me something. I was almost hyperventilating when the woman behind the counter said something. His eyes held mine for a second more before he turned his attention back to her, his lips stretching back into a smile. Regaining my sense of self I dropped my head down to the ground and walked quickly, but stiffly to the door. Once in the hall, I practically flew out of the main building doors and out into the dreary October day.

The cool air felt good on my face. I slowed my pace trying to calm my racing heart. I wasn't in any hurry to get back to home and walking was always a good way for me to think, so I headed toward the commons. It was a decent stretch and my stomach had been grumbling since morning. Even though my nerves were still humming with the electricity of realizing he wasn't just a figment of my imagination, I was starving. I've always been small, but my voracious appetite made up for my size, especially when I was stressed. It seems to grow exponentially any time I'm nervous or stressed. I hoped they were still serving breakfast because I was definitely craving a full meal of fluffy pancakes soaked in butter and syrup, the kitchen's famous scrambled cheddar cheese eggs, and bacon.

The air was just starting to mist when I opened the door to the commons. I was immediately greeted by the warm aroma of maple syrup and bacon as it wafted from the cafeteria. My stomach answered with another low rumble. The breakfast hour was almost over considering it was almost eleven so there were only a few students in line and a couple handfuls crowded around some of the small round tables, the day's newspaper sprawled out in front of them. I focused on my breakfast mission trying to ignore the few people who were staring at me. I've learned over time to just focus on menial things and block out the people around me. I've noticed that the older people get the better they are at controlling their emotions. Now that I'm in college, they still stare but they're usually not as obvious about it as when I was in high school.

I grabbed a tray, set a roll of silverware on it and proceeded to slide the tray down the sleek metal bars, looking through the glass panels, hunting for what I wanted. Once my plate was stuffed I reached into the drink cooler next to the end of the food line for a bottle of orange juice and turned toward the cashier. I paid and began scanning for a place to sit. I searched for somewhere secluded enough so no one would bother me; I needed time to process. I ended up next to the window farthest from the door I'd come in. It was nice to be close to the rain as it pelted the glass. I always found the sound comforting for some reason.

I shoveled small bits of the cheesy eggs mixture onto my fork, twisting the melted cheddar around the end before popping it into my mouth. I chewed slowly, taking in the day's events. My first conclusion was that I had truly seen the same person in the library that I had seen again today in the administrator's office. Thinking about him again made my heart skip. I was absolutely positive he was the same person. I was also positive that he was every bit as breathtaking as he'd been the night before. My second thought was that I was going to have to repeat the process of telling my story again and I had no one to complain to and confide in about my second sighting because although Erin had a cell phone, it would probably be off for the weekend and I didn't want to bother her anyway.

So, there I was sopping up the pool of syrup with a bite-sized, skewered stack of pancakes, sulking when I glimpsed a tray slide onto the table directly in front of me. I glanced up to see Chase grinning at me as he pulled a chair out to sit. Chase was tall and built from head to toe, which was expected since he was ranked in the top ten in the state for college weightlifting. He had brown hair and equally brown eyes that complimented his tan skin. We'd known each other since the first time we'd built mud castles together behind our houses that sat side by side. We'd attended the same schools and watched each other go through all the awkward stages of growing up, which is probably why we'd never dated. Chase was also much like Erin in the sense that he was a socialite who wanted to keep his options open with a "few" too many girlfriends. Don't be fooled though, he wasn't just a jock. Beneath all that muscle was a truly intelligent human being.

"Eating a late breakfast I see." Still grinning, he bit off a chunk of his chicken sandwich while shaking his protein shake. They'd switched to lunch while I'd been sitting there. I peeked at the clock on the wall, it was almost one. How had I been there so long?

I mustered up a small smile, "Yeah, I've had a busy morning." I took a sip of my orange juice.

He gulped a swig of his shake and winked at me, "Or was it just a busy night." I smiled wider. Chase was always good at lifting my spirits when everything was amuck.

I chuckled, "Maybe for you playboy, but *I* was busy studying." I bit off a piece of bacon that had gone soggy after sitting for too long.

He shrugged, "If that's what they're calling it now, then I guess I was busy studying too, a couple of times." He took another bite of his sandwich.

I sighed. "Yeah, real funny," I said and chewed on another bite of gummy textured bacon.

He cleared his throat, "But, seriously though, you're just now starting to study?"

I rolled my eyes. "I thought that was the whole point of college, to cram right before the tests that decide whether you have a chance of actually passing the class. Is everyone else so prepared, or just you?" I paused, still chewing, "And no, I didn't just start studying, give me some credit, midterms do start on Monday. I'd be an idiot to only give myself two days of study time." Truth was I was giving myself about four, but there wasn't a chance I'd admit to it.

He'd gulped down the last of his shake during my little rant. His eyes narrowed on my face while he smirked.

"Uh-huh. Well, as long as you believe that story, that's all that matters. Either way, good luck, and if you need any help you know I'm there." This was one of the many reasons why Chase and I were best friends; he was there whenever I needed him, no matter what. I could remember the time in high school when my first boyfriend dumped me; he wasn't really my boyfriend, since he admitted he was only taking me out because of a dare. Like I said I wasn't very popular. I'd called Chase moping about the whole ordeal. He'd shown up fifteen minutes later with a tub of strawberry ice cream, my favorite. Little did I know that he had been on a date himself. After I'd cried until my eyes were red he had confessed that she wasn't the smartest cheerleader on the squad. He had dropped her off at home after feigning a sudden case of nausea. I smiled now remembering how he'd turned that night around for me.

"You missed out on a good party," he added absently.

"Yeah, there were still people at the house last night when I got home after midnight."

"So, what simultaneously managed to keep you so busy this morning and get you down?" He'd finished eating and had slid his tray to the side. He was rotating his empty shake cup between his fingertips.

I shrugged, not really wanting to recite the details of my story for the third time today.

I leaned forward a little. "Did you hear about the murder?"

He nodded.

"I was at the library last night shortly before it happened."

His eyes tightened the slightest bit as he focused on my face, the cup now motionless in his hands.

"You're kidding me. Did you see anything, anybody? Why were you walking around campus so late by yourself?" He leaned forward so that we were inches apart, his face serious, waiting for my response.

I sighed, looking everywhere but his face as I said, "No, I didn't see anything, there was a guy on the top floor that I saw briefly. I was studying. You know I can't concentrate through one of Erin's parties."

I managed to leave out the details that the guy was almost painfully beautiful. I didn't need Chase haggling me when Erin was already good enough at that.

His lips that had been pressed together into a tight line while listening to my explanation eased the slightest bit before he started to speak. He was preparing to give me the "it's not safe, be careful speech". I could feel it. I groaned inwardly.

"Yeah, I know Ansley, but you shouldn't be walking the campus so late. You don't know who that guy could've been." His face was troubled. "I know you're not going to listen to me on this, so just promise me you'll call if you see him again on one of your late night treks."

He unleashed his pitiful pleading face on me before I nodded in mute agreement. We spent the rest of our lunch catching up on the newest campus gossip and his new girlfriend.

I opened the door to leave the commons glancing at the clock on my way out. It was 3:22pm. The rain had dwindled to a light drizzle. The misty wet swirled my hair so that it clung to my head, soaking my sweatshirt by the time I reached my jeep. I turned on the windshield wipers, listening to them squeak across the glass as I drove home.

I ran toward the house, my jeans like wet weights and my shoes squeaking and sloshing as my feet smacked the ground. By the time I reached the front porch I was worn, but my spirits sank even lower when I saw a man sitting motionless on the bench swing, watching my failing attempt to shake the water off my soppy jeans.

His eyes brightened as he smiled. "Ms. Welsh I'm guessing?"

I stood there dripping but mustered up a weak smile and nodded.

He walked over and extended his hand. "Detective Madison. Do you mind if I ask you a few questions?"

He was dressed in a suit that resembled that of a detective. The jacket and pants were a drab gray. He had a pressed, crisp white shirt underneath, black leather shoes, and a silver badge hanging on his matching black leather belt. Although he dressed the part, he didn't look anything like a detective, more like a high class bouncer or bodyguard. I wondered how he managed to stay dry since he wasn't carrying a raincoat. He must have been waiting for me for quite some time. He looked to be in his early thirties although his head was shaved and shiny in the resemblance of a newly polished bowling ball. He was short, but not stocky, with a warm, friendly smile.

I shook his hand and nodded again. "I don't mind."

His smile grew wider as he pulled out a little pad of paper and pen.

I pulled out my keys and unlocked the door. Besides Webster patiently waiting by the door the house was empty, quiet. I looked around the impeccably clean rooms as I led him to the kitchen. Scott must be coming over tonight to pick her up. I smiled, imagining Erin running around trying to clean, which was something she absolutely loathed.

I pulled out a chair at the small square wooden table that usually served host as a poker table. Detective Madison pulled out the chair across from me, sat down, and laid his notepad on the hard surface, the pen poised between his fingers ready and waiting.

He cleared his throat. "So Ms. Welsh, I've gathered that you were at the library last night?" It was more of an assumption than a question.

"Around eleven, not much later." I grabbed the bottom of my sweatshirt and pulled it over my head. It was damp, so the semi-cool air blowing from the vents was making me shiver. I'd have to remember to turn the fan off and the heat on. Erin always kept it freezing in here.

His pen swiveled across the miniature notepad. "Notice anything out of the ordinary?" He paused briefly, his eyes making contact with mine.

I began pulling my hair back to tie it up because now the ends were dripping water through my thin shirt, causing it to cling to my back.

"Right before I left I saw a guy on the fifth floor."

The pen raced across the paper, his eye brows knit together in concentration.

He didn't look up from writing as he asked, "Can you describe him for me?"

I nervously tucked a few of the loose strands that had escaped the band behind my ear. "He was tall, had on jeans and a dark shirt, I think. He had dark hair and eyes." *He was breathtaking.*

"Anything else you can tell me about him?" He pressed, questioning eyes searching my face.

I shook my head. "No, not that I can remember. I was really tired."

He wrote a few more lines, closed the pad, and stuck it and the pen in his jacket pocket.

He pulled his wallet from a hidden inner compartment of his jacket and sighed as he took out his business card.

"Here's my card. The number to the station and my cell are on the back. If you can think of anything else please don't hesitate to call."

I took the card, nodding.

His lips pressed together as his eyes searched my face. "I shouldn't be telling you this, but for some reason I think you should know. The girl wasn't just mauled," he paused, taking a deep breath before continuing, "she didn't have a single drop of blood in her body. She was covered with bruises, cuts, and what appear to be crude bite marks. The autopsy couldn't really negate or prove anything which is one of the reasons it has yet to be released to the press." He pinched the bridge of his nose between his thumb and forefinger for a few moments before returning his pleading eyes to me.

"I'm just warning you to be careful. So far you're the only person who has come forward with any information. I don't know if whoever or whatever the attacker was knows that you were in the area or not. You have my number, call if you need anything." He nodded stiffly in confirmation.

I shivered, whether it was because my clothes were sticking to me like a cold second skin or because of this newly acquired knowledge, I didn't know.

Chapter 2: The Statue

ॐ

It was close to five when Detective Madison left. I heaved myself up to my room to change out of my sopping wet clothes. Webster had just snuck in through the crack of my door, weaving his onyx body through the thin crevice, when I heard Erin burst through the front door muttering how late she was as she ran up the stairs to start packing furiously. I was finishing working through the wet snarls of my hair with my brush as I made my way to her room.

"Forgot to pack?" I asked as I sprawled out on her bed to watch her throw jumbled clothes into a duffle bag. She rolled her eyes, still scrambling around the room, gathering up miscellaneous items she needed for her trip.

"Yeah, and he's going to be here any minute."

"Need help with anything?"

"No, I think I've pretty much got it all."

The doorbell rang and I looked over to Erin who was now looking for something under her bed. I got up and hurried downstairs, opening the door to find a tall, blonde haired, blue eyed and well built, guy patiently waiting.

He smiled, flashing his perfect white teeth, "Hi, is Erin here?"

"Yep, you must be Scott."

"You guessed right," he replied as his smile widened.

"I'm Ansley and Erin's just finishing getting ready." I stepped aside gesturing for him to come in and peered up the stairs, looking for any sign that she was ready.

"So, you're the infamous roommate with beautiful green eyes." He looked at me, but not the way other guys did. He wasn't staring or acting funny. I felt normal, just like I did when I was around Erin.

"I don't know about infamous, but roommate with green eyes, sure enough," I said looking toward the stairs again. No sign of Erin.

"I've only seen one other person with eyes the color of yours," he added quietly, his smile still pasted on. I smiled in return, feeling confused as I shifted from foot to foot uneasily. I glanced up at the stairs again. Erin was almost to the bottom step. Her features brightened at the sight of Scott as she balanced the strap of her bag on her shoulder.

"Don't have too much fun tonight," she said, winking as she hurried by me.

"You either," I said, smiling wryly. She stuck her tongue out at me as she closed the door behind her. I liked seeing her happy. As the door clicked shut I wondered what Scott meant with the whole green eyes bit. I'd have to ask Erin later.

I popped a frozen lasagna dinner into our tiny microwave and pulled my books out from my pack. I scattered them across the kitchen table, my mood uplifted after seeing Erin in such high spirits. I ate slowly as I sank into my studies.

The smell of garlic still lingered as I sat hunched over my history book and felt my eyes begin to droop. I looked at the microwave's digital clock, and let out a deflated sigh when I realized it was only 8:30. I had to get up and move around. Maybe a change of atmosphere would help.

I knew I was going to go to the library even before I started looking for my pepper spray. As I was flat out on my stomach, arm fully extended under the bed, my fingers hunting for the small round bottle, I went through all the reasons why what I was about to do was a bad idea. They were all legitimate reasons that I normally would have listened, but I wanted to go for a drive and was tired of feeling afraid. My fingers curled around the black and red can as I dragged it from under the bed. Everything was going to be just fine. I called Chase and left him a message telling him where I was going in case anything happened then slid on my boots and leather jacket. There was a good chance the temperature had dropped considerably after the day's rain. After filling my canvas pack full of books, I grabbed my wallet and keys and strode out the door, my energy level already improved.

The air was even cooler than last night, but it felt good on my face. I walked down the few wooden steps and the short brick walk to my jeep. I revved the engine a few times, warming it up before shifting to first and speeding off toward campus.

I had a new sense of freedom walking in the open night. The faint beat of music from a nearby dorm thumped in the distance, giving me comfort that I wasn't alone. With my arms swinging purposefully by my sides, I held my pepper spray ready, my finger poised on the button.

When I opened the library door I let out a breath of relief I hadn't realized I'd been holding. As I climbed the last few steps I concluded that the trip was worth it. I was happy to be out of the house and in a place where I could concentrate better. I sprawled my books and papers across a long wooden table and sat down for a few hours of studying.

I was finally working on literature, with only the quiet hum of the heater and the scratch of my pencil across the paper when I felt a light wisp of air brush my hair. My pencil froze in place. It was after hours which meant it was highly unlikely that anyone else would be here. I felt like a child hiding her head under the covers, trying to decide whether or not it was safe to peek out from her fluffy shelter.

My heart was already racing when I slowly lifted my head. I suddenly felt it skip, stop and restart trying to pound itself out of my chest.

He was standing in the same spot as the night before, like a perfectly sculpted statue, wearing dark jeans and a blood red colored shirt that stretched across his chest. His head was slightly lowered as he gazed at me from under his dark lashes. His expression held the same troubled curiosity.

Oddly enough, my fear dissolved as soon as I saw him. But I couldn't think of what to do. I felt like I would crumble to dust if he disappeared again.

"Hi," I said before I could stop myself.

He blinked a few times, as if waking from a daze before his eyebrows creased together. All the while the rest of his body stayed completely motionless. I sat as still as possible, afraid if I moved he would cease to exist.

His face slowly started to relax as he breathed a wary, "Hello." His voice was quiet and smooth with a rough tinge on the edges that was magnified by the library's thick silence. His eyes flickered to the pencil in my hand that had started to tremble. The expression on his face shifted.

"I'm sorry. I didn't mean to frighten you," he added quietly.

I stumbled over my response as the words came out in a jumble, "Oh...you didn't...I'm not scared, just tired from studying...you know with midterms starting on Monday." I mentally slapped myself for sounding like a complete moron.

I knew I should pack my stuff and casually leave, my senses were screaming that something was wrong, that I should be afraid.

His lips twitched, fighting a smile, "You should be." His tone was serious. "You're alone?" he asked.

"Yes," I responded before pressing my lips together in regret. Why did I tell him that? You don't tell a strange guy you're alone where no one can hear you scream. Ugh! He waited, quietly watching my mental squabble, amusement highlighting his features.

"Not wise on your part. He followed you here and was waiting for you outside until he saw me. He's left for now but I'm sure he'll return," he finally said before falling silent, his eyes studying me.

Did he read my mind? No, that was crazy, impossible. I shifted in my chair, uncomfortable by the sudden turn in the conversation. He stiffened, his eyes suddenly flaring, intense as they followed my movement. I tucked a strand of hair behind my ear.

His eyes closed as he inhaled and quietly whispered, "I can see now that this might not have been the best idea."

In those few brief moments I thought I saw his face grow even paler. I squinted my eyes before blinking a few times, trying to clear my vision. That couldn't have possibly happened.

He stood there a moment longer before swiftly turning to leave.

I desperately searched for something to say, to keep him here just a little longer. "Thank you, I guess...for being here."

Still walking, he turned his head to say, "You're welcome," over his shoulder before he was gone. The door to the stairs slowly closed behind him. I sat there, staring blankly.

I decided to give up on studying and began gathering up my things, lost in a mix of emotions. I was annoyed because I'd wanted him to stay and couldn't figure out what was so wrong with me that he didn't want to talk to me. I was confused as to how he knew who the so called attacker was, and I was deeply afraid from the sudden realization that I now had to walk back to my jeep, *alone*.

I simultaneously slid on my jacket and rummaged through my bag for my phone. Once my fingers found the sleek silver device, I pulled it open and punched in Chase's number.

He answered on the second ring. "Ansley? You okay?" I could hear the booming music and the dull roar of voices in the background. He must be at a party.

"Yeah, I'm fine. Hey, would you mind meeting me at the library and walking me back to my jeep?"

I could hear the smile in his voice. "Wouldn't mind at all. Get a little spooked did we?"

I let out a sigh, but couldn't keep the corners of my mouth from pulling up.

"Something like that. See you in a few?"

I could hear the music and voices fade as he walked outside. "See you in a few," he replied before we simultaneously hung up.

As I made my way down the five flights of stairs I continued to run what had happened through my head. He was paler tonight and still incredibly handsome. My heart jumped at the thought of him standing there, the way his lips twitched, amused by some inner joke, how his eyes seemed to change, and the soft purr of his voice. I was still trying to figure out why exactly he'd been there when I pushed open the heavy glass doors to see Chase quietly leaning against the wall.

As soon as he turned his head, I could see his eyes light up slightly as he flashed me a wide grin. "For a second there I thought I was going to have to climb all those stairs to get you," he said in mock horror.

I rolled my eyes and smiled. "You sure got here fast." We descended the long stretch of concrete steps.

He shrugged. "Just another dorm party. I find rescuing you a lot more interesting." He nudged me with his elbow.

"Rescuing? Who said I needed rescuing? I just wanted someone to talk to on my short walk to the parking lot." I attempted a serious tone, but failed when his light chuckle made me smile.

He winked. "So, what's got you all bent out of shape that you need an escort?"

We were walking slowly side by side, my arm laced through his at the elbow. To the outside person we probably resembled a couple on a cozy date. I didn't care because it felt safe, the warm heat radiating from his body kept the cool air on my face from making me shiver.

"Oh, nothing. I just didn't feel comfortable walking alone after I really started thinking about last night."

I couldn't tell Chase that I'd seen *him* again. He'd want to know every detail and then give me some long speech about late night trips to the library and how dangerous they are. With my luck he'd also want to go looking for the guy. I had a feeling that was something Chase shouldn't do. I was tired and wanted little more than to put on my comfy sweats, slide under my covers, and sleep.

He raised an eyebrow. "It took you a walk to the library and a few hours of studying to come to this conclusion." It was more of a statement than a question.

I shrugged, not wanting to explain. "Something like that." Why was Chase always so keyed in?

We stopped walking when we reached my jeep. The fluorescent lights shone on the half full parking lot creating shadows and an eerie, hollow feel.

He smiled. "Alright, well, don't have too much fun tonight. *I* have got a party to get back to."

I nodded, smiling. "Thanks for walking with me," I said and opened my door, tossing my bag in the passenger's seat.

He shrugged. "Don't mention it, it's what I do." He turned, heading in the direction of the music.

After making my way home I walked up to the dark house missing Erin, but at the same time I was glad that I had free roam and could be alone. I needed to think about the strange, yet incredibly stunning person I kept running into at the library. Webster greeted me at the front door with a quiet meow as he weaved between my legs. I guess I wasn't entirely alone. I rubbed his head before shuffling to the kitchen to check his food and water.

After brushing my teeth and changing into my sweats, I climbed into bed. I lay awake, my thoughts streaming. Of course I couldn't quit thinking about *him.* His hair had been that same disheveled style, silk strands tossed and falling carelessly over his forehead like he'd just been running. Every time I would get close to sleep my mind would drudge up flashes of his smooth skin or the way he gazed at me. It was past one when I finally drifted into a dark hole of dreams full of him.

I was bundled tightly in a blanket on the front porch swing reading on Sunday afternoon when Scott and Erin drove up the short driveway in a shiny silver truck. I looked up from my book long enough to see them lean toward one another for a kiss. I waited to hear the truck's door open and close as I stared at the page I'd been reading. The minutes ticked by. I guess it was a *very* good weekend. When I finally heard the truck shift into reverse I stole a glance up and a small wave as Scott backed down the driveway. Erin walked toward me, her cheeks rosy and smiling. I squeezed the blanket around me trying to keep the pocket of warmth I'd created from seeping out as I stood to follow her inside the house knowing she'd want to spill every detail about her trip. I mm'd and aw'd at the correct times while my mind wandered over other things. I desperately wanted to go to the library tonight, not to study, but in hopes that I would see him again. After a day's worth of arguing with myself, I settled on staying in since I had an early morning of exams and didn't want to push my luck. It had begun raining anyway. That night, I crawled into bed in hopes that I would fall straight to sleep but even the light drum of rain outside my window that would have normally set me straight to sleep offered little help to my restless night of tossing and turning.

I woke the next morning to a dark glow that draped the room in gloomy shadows. I looked out the window to see rolls of heavy clouds suspended lifeless on a backdrop of a deep charcoal gray. It was going to be a wet, soggy day, and cold to boot. I wasn't complaining really. I enjoyed the rainy cold of Corvallis. I was always comforted by the rain.

I rubbed my eyes, yawning as I painstakingly pulled myself out of the comforts of sleep. I wasn't looking forward to the day. My first class wasn't until nine so I had an hour to get ready. Although I jumped in for a quick shower, I found myself relaxing and enjoying a few extra minutes as the warm water ran down my back. The sweet smell of my pear flavored soap mixed with the thick steam that was quickly clouding the bathroom. I toweled off and brushed my teeth.

The shower took a little longer than I expected so I was short on time. I threw on a pair of jeans and a shirt and grabbed a long, knit sweater. It happened to be one of my favorites because it hung down past my knees which helped keep me warm. It was also a pale cream color, so it went with pretty much anything. Tucking my wallet in my back pocket, I threw my pack over my shoulder and headed downstairs. Erin always stayed in a deep slumber during my morning routine. She slept like the dead. Lucky for her, she scheduled her classes for the evening because I don't think even the annoying blare of an alarm clock could wake her.

Halloween was only a couple of weeks away so I didn't expect any warm spurts in the weather. Sure enough, I was greeted by the crisp morning air as I strolled toward my jeep. I looked down the length of the quiet street lined with houses that all looked different, but in a way much the same. They were all trimmed with an antique appearance, all ranging in various sizes. Some were even three stories high. Each had a large front porch either covered in greenery or decorated with a simple swing or a few rocking chairs.

As I drove, I let the heater run full blast, fanning my hair out over my shoulders and back, running my fingers to the ends determined to get it dry. I was fortunate enough to have hair like my mother, which dried in long graceful waves when I didn't speed dry it straight with a blow dryer. By the time I reached the crowded parking lot my hair was barely even damp. I grabbed my pack and strode quickly up the concrete path toward the history building.

The large halls were busy with activity as students weaved in and out of one another on their way to class. I'd noticed my first few days on this campus that all the buildings smelled faintly of fresh paint. It reminded me of when I was younger. The halls in my little elementary school had smelled the same. I opened the door for American History and closed it behind me while smiling at Dr. Hartley, a short, stout man with a goatee and stubby hair that was quite rapidly turning to a dusty gray. He had a sense of humor, unlike most professors, and a warm smile.

I scanned the room for a place to sit. The desks were arranged in a stadium seating formation. I headed for the very top, which also meant the very back. I liked having a full view of the room and wasn't very comfortable with people behind me.

It was only a few minutes before class which meant the room was about half full. I imagine it was the same at every college campus, students arriving right when class starts. It seemed rude to me, but who was I to say anything about it.

I pulled my notebook out of my bag and laid it on the desk. My pen was still tucked inside the plastic fold. I took it out and clicked it, placing it on the ringed stack of scribbled notebook paper. I listened as the door opened and closed a few more times. The seats around me began to creak as they filled, the room beginning to hum with conversation. When I looked up, it was practically full. As I sat there slowly surveying my surroundings I noticed a dark shadow out of the corner of my eye. I turned to see what it was and found myself staring into a pair of midnight blue eyes.

He was leaning back in the chair with his legs stretched out in front of him, a notebook with blank paper open on his desk, his pale hands resting on it. His dark hair swept across his forehead while a smile played on his flawless lips. His eyes held something different. Was it amusement?

"My name is Morgan. I failed to introduce myself the other night. You must be Ansley."

I sat there, dazed. How did he know my name and why was he suddenly talking to me as if he'd known me more than the few brief moments we'd stared at one another? Morgan. He had a name and it fit perfectly.

He was waiting for me to say something.

"H-how do you know who I am and why are you here so late in the semester? Midterms start today," I stuttered.

He chuckled lightly, flashing his perfect white teeth. "I imagine a number of people at this school know who you are and I'm pretty sure I'll have some leeway with the exam."

I frowned. "No. What I meant was, how do you know my name?"

His lips twitched upward widening his smile slightly. "It's printed on the inside cover of your notebook." He reached over to tap the corner of plastic where I'd scribbled my name in black magic marker before returning his hand back to its place on his desk. The small movement made my heart flutter.

"Oh." I felt like an idiot. I repositioned myself in my chair, feeling awkward.

Fortunately, Dr. Hartley called the class to attention. He stood in front of his desk a hand in each of his pockets preparing to give what was probably a legendary exam speech.

"I have a few rules for taking this exam." He cleared his throat, "They are: nothing on your desk except for a pencil or pen, whichever you prefer; cell phones off; no cheating unless you're sure the person you're cheating off is sure of the answer." He raised an eyebrow toward the class, "So, no cheating. Yes, you must take the exam and no I will not give you the answers."

He paused, his face turning serious, "Unless you pay me twenty dollars per question." He looked around the classroom. A student in the front row actually pulled out a few twenties from his wallet.

Dr. Hartley shook with laughter. "I'm kidding Mr. Garrett, put your money away."

The class laughed in unison including the student who was stuffing his money back in his wallet.

Dr. Hartley sighed, shaking his head. "There's always one. Where was I? Oh yes, I'm going to pass around answer sheets and your exam booklets. You have ninety minutes, good luck." He turned to pick up a stack of papers sitting on his desk and began handing them out.

I was acutely aware of Morgan sitting next to me. It almost felt like an invisible electric field was between us, the static tickling the hair on my arms making it stand on end. I glanced over to see him tense, his fingers curled into a fist, as if he were feeling the same thing.

I was handed an exam booklet. I opened the flimsy paper cover and looked down at the first question. It all seemed foreign, as my mind suddenly went blank. I couldn't concentrate. I had studied, I knew the answers, but every part of me was more concerned with wanting to look at Morgan, wanting to see his perfect lips curve into a smile that seemed too familiar, wanting to touch his smooth, pale skin. I had to concentrate. I took a deep breath as I read the first question again, squinting as I focused my mind on what I was reading. I sat there for a second as it started to click in my mind, my pencil slowly transferring the information onto the paper. This was how the test continued, look at a question, fight every urge to look at, talk to, and touch the person next to me, breathe to try and clear my head, answer and read on to the next question.

Morgan finished his test, stood in one graceful movement, went to the front of the room to hand it in and was out the door. I sat there staring blankly at the seat he'd occupied, my mind trying to comprehend everything. Needless to say, I was one of the very last to finish. I walked to the front of the room and handed it in, distracted, my mind still wandering.

As I opened the main door to the history building, the fresh air cheered me. It felt good to be done with that test, to be outside in the open. My next class didn't start until one, so I had about an hour and a half to kill. Food seemed like a good pastime as my stomach answered with a low rumble. I turned and headed toward the commons. The campus was busy with students today. I wasn't looking forward to milling through all the people, but I needed to eat something before my next exam.

I opened the door to the commons and was met by the dull roar of voices. The cafeteria and commons area was packed with students. I decided the best thing to do was get my food, eat, and get out as soon as possible. I headed for the lunch bar, grabbed a tray and set of silverware. I picked a turkey sandwich, an orange and a random drink from the cooler at the end of the bar. I didn't care what it was as long as it was carbonated and sweet. Once I paid the clerk I scanned for somewhere to sit. My odds looked bleak; the lunch area was practically full. My eyes caught a flash of golden blonde hair as Erin waved at me from a table in the center of the large room, her bright smile welcoming. I trudged over to the table, not wanting to sit in a place so open and surrounded.

"Hey you, have a seat." She pulled out the chair next to her. I slid into it, gently setting my tray on the table.

She motioned to the group of people that I'd just joined, "Everyone remembers Ansley right?" They nodded, a few not even glancing in our direction they were so deeply involved in their conversation. Others offered a brief smile, but quickly turned back to whom they were talking with. At least they were being semi-polite.

"Everyone is talking about the murder," Erin said.

I didn't feel like trying to explain to her that most people didn't talk to me. I simply nodded, twisting the cap off my soda and putting it to my lips to gulp down a few swigs. I was worn out from thinking so much and didn't really feel like talking.

Erin appraised me with skeptical eyes as she skewered the green beans on her plate, poking them one by one, adding them to her fork until she had enough for a mouthful.

"You okay? You look kind of beat? How'd your exam go?"

"Yeah, I'm beat. That one drained me and I'm definitely not looking forward to trig. But, I guess it went okay." Minus the fact that I couldn't concentrate the tiniest bit because the most visually fascinating person I had ever seen had been sitting next to me.

"You?" I took a bite of my sandwich before I started peeling my orange.

She opened her mouth to speak, but paused, a frown forming on her face. She leaned a little closer, dropping her head slightly so that she was level with me. "Hey, do you know who that guy is who keeps looking over here?"

My eyes automatically shot up, searching for the person she was talking about. He was sitting by the window, close to where I had sat a few days before. His eyes held mine briefly before I dropped my head. The expression on his face was serious, almost angry, devoid of any of the amusement he'd had earlier.

I took in a labored breath, "Stop staring at him Erin."

She looked at me, then down at her plate of food. "Huh, wonder why he's sitting with the Dean. Seems odd doesn't it?"

She tried to keep her tone light, but I could hear something underneath, it sounded irritated.

I reflexively looked up again. He was looking at the Dean this time as they leaned toward each other, their lips moving fast, their faces stiff.

I looked back down at my orange before I could be caught in his eyes again. My fingers were wet with juice that had seeped out when my nails had accidentally cut its fleshly core. Great, now my hands were going to smell like citrus for the rest of the day. Erin interrupted my thoughts, "I've got to go Ansley. I'll catch you later. Good luck in Trig."

"Thanks, same to you," I mumbled.

I looked at her tray as she was picking it up to swiftly walk away. It was still almost full, her food barely touched which was odd because she always ate; her appetite was just as crazy as mine. She didn't look sick. Something seemed off but I couldn't put my finger on what.

I finished my sandwich in a few quick bites and gulped down the rest of my soda, leaving the mutilated orange on my plate. I didn't want to stay any longer than I had to. I risked another glance in the direction of Morgan and the Dean and found them in the same positions, completely engrossed in their conversation.

I walked out of the commons with almost a half hour remaining before my next class. I decided a little extracurricular reading wouldn't hurt as I made my way to the math building.

The structure of the math building was square in almost every way. Each angle was cut to a perfect edge. The halls were wide with bland walls and square tile floors. The double doors to the classrooms formed a perfect square shape. It all fit together like a puzzle. It definitely felt like a math building with its hollow rooms. There weren't any posters on the walls or medieval decorations like those in the history and literature buildings. The science building even had more going for it with the periodic table hanging in most classrooms and little glass beakers and measuring utensils littering the rooms. The math building was empty. Cold. Hard, plastic seats, a big desk in front and a long rectangular white board were the only attractions in the math classrooms. But I could be biased; I hated math.

I opened the door to the trigonometry classroom. It was empty, silent. I slowly climbed the wide steps to my signature seating in the top, very back. I flopped down in the chair, searched through my pack for my book, pulled it out, and let my bag drop to the floor.

I had recently borrowed *The Picture of Dorian Gray* from the campus library. It was different from the scary stories I usually read so I'd decided to give it a try. As to be expected, the book was well used. The cover was faded, the corners were creased, and the pages were soft with velvet edges, made smooth by the years of use and the many hands that had brushed them. I loved it.

I was lost in the book when I heard the door open. I glanced up to see Professor Hawkins walk in with a stack of papers in her arms. She staggered over to her desk and heaved them onto it in one quick motion then turned to the white board to grab the marker from its metal shelf. Each letter made a little squeak as she wrote in short, fast movements, her letters sharp and precise like her appearance.

Professor Hawkins was one of the younger instructors. She had shoulder length, auburn hair that she straightened every day; no piece dared to stick out of place. Her make up was always carefully applied so that all the shades blended perfectly. She always dressed chic, like she'd been plucked from the page of a popular fashion magazine. Her teaching style was much the same. Formulas were laid out meticulously and equations were calculated precisely. To her, everything was simple and understandable with lines and numbers.

The door opened again as students poured through. I looked at the clock which read five minutes to one. I quickly finished the section I was reading. The room was almost completely full when I looked up, closing my book to tuck it away. My eyes skimmed the large area. I was looking for Morgan, but I didn't know why. There were plenty of math classes at many different times. It wasn't likely that he would be in this one. Part of me desperately hoped to see him sitting in one of the small desks, while part of me knew that I was being ridiculous for wanting something so silly. I didn't see him anywhere. I felt the balloon of hope in my chest deflate. I pushed the thought aside telling myself that

I needed to concentrate anyway. Trigonometry wasn't my best subject.

Professor Hawkins didn't feel the need to explain her rules. Unlike Dr. Hartley, she had no sense of humor. As she began passing out the tests she nodded her head toward the board, "Your parameters are posted on the board. Please follow them." She continued to hand out the exam, the stack in her arms quickly shrinking.

My eyes scanned the long white panel which read:

NO TALKING
NO CELL PHONES
90 MINUTES
HAND IN WHEN FIMSHED

I sighed. I wasn't looking forward to this one. Thankfully, I was able to focus, so it didn't take nearly as long as I'd thought it would. I placed it on her desk when I finished and made my way back to my jeep. The campus was full of energy, students milling around the grounds. It looked like any ordinary college campus. A few guys were tossing a football around, another circle of students were sitting bundled up in the grass, books sprawled out in what looked to be a study group, a few other students were scattered leaning against a tree or stretched out on their backs listening to music. You would never guess that a murder had been committed just a few days ago.

Only a few heads turned when the engine of my rust bucket finally turned over with a loud barking rumble. I hastily shifted to reverse and lurched out of the parking lot toward home.

Back at home I opened my bedroom door, slid off my pack and hung my knit sweater on the chair in front of my desk. Webster was curled up comfortably on the center of my bed. I lightly nudged him aside as I crawled onto the covers. He grumbled as he resituated himself next to me. I was exhausted and fell head first into a deep slumber.

When I woke the sun was casting a deep orange glow into the room. I blinked, letting my eyes adjust to the shadows. I glanced at my alarm clock. *Crap!* It was past five and I had to be at the library at 5:30. I jumped up and scrambled to the bathroom.

I squeezed some toothpaste onto my brush and hastily scrubbed my teeth with one hand while I ran my hairbrush through my hair with the other. Rinsing my mouth, I pulled my hair back into a ponytail and splashed some cold water onto my face. I patted dry and slapped on a little make up. After doing a quick once over in the mirror I grabbed my leather jacket, threw my pack over my shoulder and ran out the front door.

The cool air slapped me in the face, finishing my not so pleasant wake up process. I pressed hard on the gas pedal, constantly checking my mirrors for any sign of cops as I sped toward the campus.

The library clock just clicked to 5:30 as I swept past a few students and behind the counter throwing Connor, the day shift clerk a quick nod. He smiled in return. "Guess I'm gone then, see you later Ansley." He collected his books and stuffed them into his book bag before turning to leave.

"Later, Connor."

I quickly logged onto the computer with my name and password. It was the library's way of keeping track of our hours. I breathed a sigh of relief as I saw that the computer's clock matched the clock on the wall. I didn't need Mrs. Shannon, the library head, upset with me for being late.

I went through my usual routine, scanning books that had been returned, organizing them on the cart by floor and then code, and then finally wheeling the heavy metal carrier around the library to place them in their homes. Thankfully tonight there weren't very many that needed to go upstairs, which was quite a workout.

By the time I finished making the rounds it was just past seven. From what I could see there were only a few students still traipsing around. I wasn't sure about the other floors though. I nestled myself into the old, rusted chair behind the counter eager to read more of my book. I was just getting to the part where the main character, Dorian Gray, curses a painting of himself and promises his soul if the painting were to grow old, letting him stay young forever, when I glimpsed movement out of the corner of my eye. I turned to see Morgan quietly observing me with a curious expression on his face. His marble skin was smooth, absent of the seriousness it had held earlier at lunch. He was wearing faded jeans and a gray hooded sweatshirt with a dark leather jacket; his hands hung loosely by his sides. He looked like a cover of GQ.

I sat there for a moment, just looking at him, my heart beating erratically. Then I realized he probably wanted help finding a book. Why else would he come to the help desk?

I met his curious eyes with mine, "Can I help you find something?"

Smiling he said, "Yes actually. I'm looking for a book, English Literature from 1800, I believe." What happened to the dark, ominous person I'd met the other night, I wondered.

I frowned. It was the same book that was required for my literature class.

His eyes searched my face as he took a step toward the counter placing his hands on the smooth surface.

"Am I annoying you?" His tone sounded amused.

I turned my head and typed the title into the computer. The floor and section number popped up immediately.

"No, I'm just trying to figure you out…I mean figure out why…are you following me?" I finished, exasperated that I couldn't form a legitimate sentence. I looked back at the computer screen to hide my frustrated face.

He chuckled quietly, "It does seem that way doesn't it? I've transferred from out of town, it's my first year." He paused and the amusement on his face dimmed slightly. "What I was wondering was, why are *you* here?" I looked up to find his intent eyes boring into mine.

I shrugged shifting my gaze away again, not really wanting to explain the details. I didn't feel like giving him the long history of how I chose to run away from all my problems. The life, the people I went to school with was what I wanted to forget, minus my parents, of course. They were good parents who let me have my space when I needed it. "It's what you do I guess, go to college, graduate, get a job." I sounded pitiful, even to myself.

"Yes, but *why* are you here?" he pressed.

"Does it matter?" I mumbled, absently clicking on the computer screen.

"I think it does." The soft tone in his voice made me turn to look at him. He waited, his expression holding something that loosely resembled compassion.

"It was expected of me. My father's an accountant, my mother's a teacher. I had no choice. So, here I am." I sighed, annoyed at myself for blurting out a loose fragment of my thoughts. Most guys left me alone. Why did he have to ask me such off the wall questions?

"You're different," he said definitively, his eyes narrowing slightly as they searched mine.

I sat there trying to figure out what he meant, my face scrunching into a frown again. "Different, like how? I'm just like every other freshman girl here, it's not like I'm a genius, or slow, or have special powers or anything."

I looked back at the computer screen confused and hurt, not knowing what he was getting at. If he meant to insult me, I'd rather he just left me alone. I decided it must be some practical joke. I tried to resist the urge to look around for a group of people watching us, waiting for the moment when they would start roaring with laughter. I failed as my eyes darted around quickly. There was no one but him and me.

I could see him grinning out of the corner of my eye. "No. Never mind. About the book though..."

He stopped, watching as I swiveled in my chair to pull out a small rectangular note card from under the counter. I scratched the floor and section number onto it.

I mustered up a weak smile, not wanting him to go, but also completely confused and frustrated by the conversation. "Let me know if you need help finding it." I said as I slid the card across the counter with my fingertips.

Slowly, his pale fingers reached out and took the card, the shift of his leather jacket the only noise to break the silence of the quiet library. I watched every movement, my heart racing faster as his hand came within inches of mine, a slow humming tingle in the space between our hands.

"Thank you," he said as he turned away toward the stairs.

"You're welcome." I sat there watching the distance between us grow as he opened the cold metal door to the stairwell and disappeared.

I groaned when he was out of sight, shaking my head at myself as I leaned back in my chair. My conversational skills had definitely seen better days. I tried to pick up where I'd left off in my book, but my mind wandered after only a few sentences. The clock above the stairwell clicked by slowly until I eventually started cataloging a pile of books that had been donated.

I nodded and smiled at a few students as they walked out of the stairwell and past the counter, but I never saw Morgan pass by the counter again. It was close to ten when I climbed the stairs to do a quick check of all the floors, making sure the building was empty. I made my way back down the five flights trying to remember if he had walked by, but I couldn't. I pushed the question aside figuring that I must have had my back turned while I was caught up in cataloging.

I turned off the computer, slid my jacket on, grabbed my bag, and headed for the main glass doors. I flipped the light switch so that only the security light above the stairwell shone brightly and closed the heavy glass door behind me. The keys clinked against each other as I locked the dead bolt.

The night was quiet as I made my way down the stairs and headed toward the parking lot. Nothing moved. There was no breeze or rustle of leaves. Everything was still, lifeless. My late night walks were always peaceful but the absence of any sound was unusual. I was mentally kicking myself for leaving the little can of pepper spray on my nightstand when I heard a low growl right behind me. Before I could react two big hands grabbed my shoulders, picked me up and hurled me to the ground. I threw my arms out instinctively to catch my fall. My palms scraped along the sidewalk painfully. I could feel the sticky, wetness of blood seeping from places where the concrete had ripped away my skin.

I was stunned, but was still trying to get my feet under me to run when I felt myself yanked up by my ponytail. I cried out in pain as a hand grasped my throat to sling me into the nearest tree. My back took the brunt of the impact, but my head started to spin from colliding with the tree. Before I had any time to move, the same hand curled around my throat again crushing me against the tree, blocking any air from moving in or out of my lungs. I tried desperately to break loose, kicking my legs and aiming for vital areas. The person me who held me looked like any typical college student. He was big and built like Chase, but with jet black hair and a pair of furious dark eyes.

My hands clawed at his fingers as I looked down at his muscular arm that was beginning to ripple and grow. His entire body started to quiver. When I looked back into his eyes they were a round, pale gold. I squirmed harder, even more afraid, but I could feel the lack of oxygen slowing me down, my nose and lips starting to tingle. I was fighting with what energy I had, frantically trying to keep my eyes open when I heard an even deeper growl, accompanied by a loud snap and then the hand that had been around my throat disappeared.

I gasped for air falling limply to the ground that swirled around me. I wanted to open my eyes, to get up and run as fast as I could, but I was afraid I'd lose the contents of my stomach if I dared to look around me. I thought I could hear two different animalistic growls off in the distance, but was too disoriented to be sure. I've really got to stop reading those horror books, I thought. My head throbbed. I tried to swallow but my throat felt thick and dry. I was certain it would be bruised. Too weak to move I decided to lay there until the ground quit moving. A moment later I heard the soft footsteps of someone approaching.

Chapter 3: Changes

I heard Morgan's soft, anxious voice by my head. "You're bleeding. Are you alright?"

My eyes flickered open to find a pair of dark blue eyes full of worry staring back at me.

"S'just my hands. I'm okay minus a little dizziness," I croaked, my throat hoarse and dry. I pushed myself up with my arms, leaning my head against the tree nearest me. I had closed my eyes to ease the spinning when I thought I felt something like ice brush lightly along my cheek. They flashed opened to look into his. His fingers gently traced a line down my cheek across the line of my jaw and lingered on my throat, his eyes narrowing before flaring with anger. The light tingle from his fingers made my stomach flip with butterflies.

"It's going to bruise," he whispered, almost impossible to hear even in the still night. I watched his jaw flex as his eyes meticulously examined my tender skin. Cool air swept over my palms as his hands searched for a place that wasn't oozing blood.

He shook his head. "Can you stand?"

I nodded weakly as I put my hands on the ground to help push myself up. I hissed in pain, the grass feeling like soft needles sticking to my scraped palms. Morgan looked at me with worry etched on his face.

"I'm fine." He slid his arm around my waist pulling me the rest of the way up in one quick motion. My head spun as I concentrated on keeping the ground level. I wasn't sure if my unsteadiness was from the attack or from being so close to Morgan. He stood next to me gently holding me in place.

"I'm taking you to the hospital," he stated, his voice calm and matter of fact.

"No. Really, I'm fine." I took a few steps forward out of his reach, thinking I could walk straight when the ground swirled up to meet me. I felt his arms around me again as he caught me in one swift, graceful movement.

"A little stubborn, aren't we?" he said, amusement in his voice.

I looked at him gritting my teeth.

His lips twitched like he was fighting laughter. "You don't have a choice," he added in an absolute tone.

I huffed, my mind suddenly flashing to the reason we were out here having this argument.

"Who or what was that?" My eyes searched his face, which became a mask of seriousness.

"Someone bent on killing you apparently," he said evasively while retrieving my pack that had been thrown next to the tree during the attack.

"No, it was something more. I saw his eyes change color and his arm…" I trailed off not wanting to relive the rest. He started pulling me along, his movement easy even though he was towing me along underneath his arm.

"I don't know what you're talking about. You must have hit your head harder than I thought."

That did it. I planted my feet, as wobbly as they were. "No," I growled, "you were here, I know it, I could feel it. What was that?"

We stood there a few moments like a couple of angry five year olds. He scowled down at me, his beautiful face creased where his eyebrows pulled together, while I frowned up at him, my hands balled into tights fists at my sides.

Finally he sighed, "Look Ansley. I'll explain, just not right now. Right now, you're going to the hospital." He eyed me warily as he waited for my response.

I waited a few more seconds before finally giving in. "Fine, but this is completely unnecessary." I looked pointedly at him. "And I won't forget, so you will be explaining sometime."

Even though I knew I'd figure out what was going on sooner or later, I couldn't stop the feeling that he could be just as stubborn as me. I stood there fighting the urge to stick my tongue out at him like a child as my flimsy legs wobbled slightly.

"Do you need me to carry you?" I could see the shadow of sarcasm on his face in the bright fluorescent lights.

"I'll walk," I grumbled.

We slowly trudged along the path in silence. What was he trying to hide? I caught myself stealing glimpses of him. His skin seemed less pale, almost flushed, and his eyes were focused like he was lost in some internal conflict. I thought I'd be warm, being so close to him, his arm wrapped securely around my waist, but he held no warmth. His skin was as cold as the cold night air where mine brushed against his.

When we reached the parking lot I tried to steer us toward my jeep, but his steel body propelled us in a different direction.

"My car is that way." I pointed to the opposite direction in which we were heading.

He smirked, "And mine is right here." We stopped at a sleek black car with dark tinted windows. I glimpsed the four small silver rings that created the emblem for Audi.

His hand dropped from my waist as he reached past me to open the passenger door. I stood there for a second gawking before I slid into the smooth leather seat. It was soft and cushiony. I inhaled the new car smell. The inside of the vehicle was just as sleek and flawless as the outside.

He was around the car, opening the door, and sliding in next to me in one fluid movement which I could swear was too fast for any normal human being. He started the car and it purred to life. His eyes connected with mine while he clicked it into reverse. That humming energy I'd noticed before radiated from him, sliding over my skin like a cool blanket. I found myself making the same comment he'd made to me earlier. "You're different."

His eyes shifted back to the road, the expression on his face suddenly tense. In one quick motion he slid the car into drive and we were speeding out of the parking lot.

"Seatbelt," he muttered as we began to speed through the night. I looked out the window watching everything outside sweep by in a dark blur.

We pulled up to the hospital and parked in record time. A drive that would have taken me forty-five minutes, he managed in only twenty. I was glad I'd never peeked at the dash to check his speed. My jeep was loud, but it lacked in the acceleration and high speed department. I'd never even gone over sixty-five miles an hour with it.

He was swiftly out and opening my door before I even unhooked my seatbelt. I looked up at him, shocked as I pulled myself onto my jello-like legs, my head barely throbbing anymore. The blood on my palms had dried, crusted into little globules. I tried to ignore them as he reached around me to close the door.

"You don't have to do this you know." I was mortified, stumbling into the emergency room looking a complete mess while the person next to me was perfection in the flesh. "I can handle it from here if you want to take off." A small part of me was hoping he would leave, so I could crawl off into some hole to hide from this embarrassment. The larger majority of me though, the part that sent butterflies racing through my stomach and fire through my veins when he gazed at me with flawless smiling lips, desperately wanted him to stay by my side.

He raised an eyebrow at me and said, "So you could sneak off and avoid this fun little trip? I don't think so." He smiled sarcastically and steered me toward the doors of the ER.

I wobbled next to him through the doors and up to the registration desk with as much dignity as I could muster. The registration desk was occupied by an older woman with round curves and soft skin that reminded me of a peach, the blush on her cheeks that same orange-red color. The lines on her face accented her subtle features and her soft white hair delicately curled around her face. She looked up at us with almond shaped eyes the color of dark amber.

"Can I help you?" Her soft voice quaked.

Morgan unleashed the full power of his smile on her. "Yes, I'm looking for Dr. Madelyn Greene. Can you let her know Morgan is here to see her?"

He asked as if he were at some elegant event looking for an old friend, instead of at the ER supporting the weight of some silly girl, which seemed completely effortless to him.

The woman behind the desk eyed me carefully then looked back to him, returning his smile. "Let me call back for her, dear."

She moved slowly reaching for the phone, to punch a few of the buttons while carefully putting the receiver to her ear. After explaining to someone that Dr. Greene was needed the woman hung up.

"She's on her way."

Morgan nodded, not moving from the desk. Less than thirty seconds later a small woman, maybe in her late twenties with curly, shoulder length brown hair and smooth, caramel colored skin walked through the big metal doors separating the waiting area from the trauma room. Everything about her outfit screamed doctor. The white medical coat, pasty green scrubs, stethoscope dangling from her neck, and squeaky tennis shoes were a dead giveaway. She was beautiful and looked to me like she was too young to be a doctor. She reminded me of the dance instructor I had when my mother was still struggling to "culture" me. I think it was her last dying attempt to get me out of reading so much. Like the instructor, Dr. Greene moved in long, graceful movements. Her lips were stretched into a bright smile as she looked us over. She held out her arms as she continued to walk forward.

"I wasn't sure that it was you. But alas, here you are. Morgan, it's so good to see you!" He managed a one arm hug while still holding me.

"You know it's been too long Mattie." They pulled away from each other's embrace before she turned to look at me, her smile still warm and welcoming.

"And who's this?" she asked, her voice sweet and light as air. I could feel his body tense the slightest bit.

"Ansley, Madelyn. Madelyn, Ansley." He paused for a moment, before continuing, "Do you think you could take a look at her? I think she might have a concussion and her hands are cut up."

She looked back at him, still smiling, but with a questioning look in her eyes. They stood there a few moments, staring at each other before she nodded. Her expression was blank as she turned her attention back to me,

"Let's get you in a room, shall we?" She said cheerfully and turned to lead us through the metal doors she'd just come from. I was ushered into a hospital bed with pastel and gray patterned curtains pulled on either side, creating the illusion of a small room. I hated hospitals more than any amount of math. They were always cold and smelled faintly of rubbing alcohol, bleach, and death.

She and Morgan disappeared while I got situated with a nurse fluttering around me. Just before slipping through the cloth partition Morgan threw me a wink and a smile. I couldn't help but smile back, finally beginning to feel safe. But then, just as the curtain settled and blocked Morgan from my view, I thought I saw a flicker of unease on his face and my smile faded as my thoughts wandered back over the strangeness of the last hour.

I was sent for x-rays and scans. The cuts on my hands were cleaned and bandaged. Eventually I was returned to my room where I waited. I laid my head back and was resting with my eyes closed when I felt the air in the room change. It felt different, almost like static. I opened them to find Morgan standing at the foot of the bed, amusement spread across his face. He slowly stepped over to the side of the bed never breaking eye contact. His face became serious as if he were concentrating, his eyebrows knitted together in frustration. He leaned closer, cautiously placing his hands lightly on either side of my head. It felt like they were humming with energy, but I'd also knocked my head against a tree so a lot of things were throbbing. I stared back into his intense eyes, confused by his actions. My heart beat faster in my chest but I remained as still as possible, focusing on the deep blue of his eyes. They weren't the color of the ocean. They were much darker than that. Like the color of the sky just after sunset when the bright purples and reds have faded. I stared, searching his eyes until I found the reflection of the bright hospital lights, creating the illusion of stars.

He suddenly pulled his hands away but kept his face close, its smoothness set like stone.

I blinked trying to bring myself back to earth. Having him so close, the air seemed fresher with his face next to mine, as if someone had opened a window to let the cool breeze settle around us.

"W-what?" I stuttered, "And why are your hands vibrating?"

He mirrored my confused expression, blinking as he leaned away slightly, surprised by my question.

"Vibrating? Explain it to me, what's it feel like?" His eyes widened, anxious for my response.

"I don't know, it's like a dull electric current or something, maybe I do have a concussion."

He leaned closer for a moment, his cool breath tickling my nose and lips.

"You remember everything that happened tonight?" he asked sounding skeptical. I hadn't hit the tree that hard, I thought.

"Yeah, why wouldn't I?" I said puzzled and feeling uneasy. Did concussions cause memory loss, was I loosing my mind? I had a pretty good memory, better than most in fact. I ran through a quick check in my head of my name and names of family members, birthdates, and such. Satisfied my mind was working just fine, I turned my attention back to Morgan.

"No reason." He leaned away from the bed, hunching his shoulders in what could only be described as a sulk. Madelyn walked through the curtain, a clipboard in hand, her features lit by a brilliant smile. Her mouth opened to speak but Morgan cut her off. "She remembers," he said quietly. Her mouth shut with an audible snap as her expression faded.

"You mean you couldn't..." she trailed off.

"Yes, that's exactly what I mean." He shook his head slowly from side to side, eyes focusing on the white tile floor.

"What do you think she is?" she whispered, still looking at him.

His eyes shot up, narrowing as he glared at her, his lips pulling back over his teeth slightly. The sudden change made me shudder.

Madelyn didn't even flinch; she merely stood there returning his stare, her face innocent.

She nodded before looking back to me, her face bright again. "Let me take a look at the bump on the back of that head of yours." She walked over to the bed, placing her clipboard on the stand next to me. Her small, warm fingers began feeling lightly along the back of my skull.

I flinched when she grazed the spot where I'd slammed into the tree.

"Tender?"

I nodded slightly.

I struggled to sit there as patiently as possible even though I had a surge of questions. I could see out of the corner of my eye that she held the same expression of concentration Morgan had when he'd been holding my head between his hands minutes before. I watched as her brows knit together and her face scrunched in the same frustrated way. She blinked a few times, her face relaxing before looking down at me.

"Can you tell me what happened tonight?" she smiled, warmth radiating from her soft features.

"I was walking home from the library when someone grabbed me and tried to choke me to death by crushing..." I trailed off, her expression making me nervous. She was looking at Morgan, his lips pressed together in a tight line while he stared back. He shook his head side to side in one quick motion. She sighed and nodded.

"Kyle and Mitch are going to have fun with this," she said. "She feels different. Blake might know." Know what? I wanted to scream. I couldn't understand what was going on.

He rolled his eyes up to the ceiling, shaking his head while blowing out a breath of air.

"I guess you're right, we'll see tomorrow." His eyes flickered to me briefly, his expression wary.

I opened my mouth to unleash the stream of questions flowing through my head when Madelyn's pager began beeping. She pulled the small black device off the band of her waist with a loud snap.

She sighed, "I've got to go. I'm needed a few rooms down." She looked at me warmly.

"Well, the good news is that your x-rays look fine." She let out a nervous laugh and cleared her throat. "You do have a minor concussion, nothing serious. So, you need to rest and you're going to be tender for a few days. Take ibuprofen for headaches and any pain. Do you have someone who can check on you every few hours?"

I nodded; Erin was always good at playing nurse.

"Okay, well it was a pleasure to meet you Ansley and good luck." She patted my shoulder lightly before dropping her eyes to the ground as she disappeared through the curtain, subtly hurrying to get out of the small room.

I looked at Morgan who was running his fingers through his dark hair, shaking his head and chuckling quietly to himself. He seemed to be doing that a lot tonight, shaking his head. I had so many questions, the feeling of them weighing me down. I opened my mouth, then snapped it shut not really knowing where to begin. I opted for something completely off subject.

"What's so funny?"

"Impossible situations...that's my specialty, getting involved in impossible situations." He shrugged.

I felt my blood heat as his remark hit my last nerve, making me furious. I slung my legs over the side of the hospital bed and strode past him through the curtain attempting to walk as straight and un-wobbly as possible. If I was such a pain, so impossible, then he should have just left me to die. He shouldn't have driven me to the hospital and shouldn't have pretended he cared. I stomped through the big metal doors into the waiting area and through the sliding glass doors into the chilly night. I turned left toward the college.

I vaguely heard someone call my name. Cool fingers wrapped around my wrist, pulling me to a stop and spinning me around. I glared up at Morgan as he stood there smiling down at me.

"Bit of a temper?" He looked as if he were on the verge of laughter. I tried to yank myself free, but although his fingers were gentle, his hold was like steel. I could feel a dull vibration radiating up my arm from his touch, making my head tingle.

"You're going to see temper if you don't let go of my wrist so that I can relieve you of your impossible situation."

This time he did laugh, throwing his head back; the sound was musical. He calmed as his eyes became suddenly intense. He gazed down at me and slowly raised his free hand to sweep a few loose strands of hair off my face. His fingers grazed my cheek, making my skin tingle as he tucked the hair gently behind my ear. I shivered, my heart fluttering, as I fought to maintain self control. His eyes shifted back to mine. The buzzing current between us increased. I leaned closer without thinking, breathing him in.

"I like impossible situations," he whispered.

I leaned a little closer, tilting my head as I reached up to place my hand gently against the side of his face. He suddenly released my wrist, taking a deep breath and a small step back, shaking his head and blinking his eyes like he was trying to wake from a deep sleep. I focused, my eyes adjusting before my face scrunched into a frown. He could see the feeling of rejection forming.

His eyes softened. "It's not safe...for you," he whispered.

I shook my head, questions crashing down on me again like a tidal wave. Why, why wasn't it safe? Enough with the cryptic answers. Before I had a chance to speak, he turned, heading toward his car.

"You coming?" he asked.

We didn't say much on the drive back. I wanted to ask him so many things, but something kept me from flooding him with the thoughts and worries that were bouncing around in my head. I let the smooth ride calm my nerves, almost rocking me to sleep as we sped down the dark road.

When he took a right instead of a left on the road leading to the college I asked, "Where are we going?" The sound of my voice in the quiet car sounded foreign.

"I'm taking you home. You shouldn't be driving with a concussion." He kept his eyes on the road.

"Don't you want directions?" I asked before he turned on the street that was just two blocks from my house. How does he know where I live? I thought.

"You've been following me?"

"On and off."

"Why?" I whispered.

He finally looked at me. "My reasons are much too complicated and dangerous for you to know or understand," he said in a dark tone. I felt the pit of my stomach freeze into a ball of ice. Everything about him clearly said danger. Perhaps I was okay with the cryptic responses to all my questions. I was suddenly unsure if I really wanted any straightforward answers.

It was after midnight when he stopped, parking in the same spot my jeep usually claimed. Again, he was around the car, pulling my door open before my seatbelt was unhooked.

We walked up the brick path, his feet falling into the same pattern as mine. When we reached the base of the steps I turned to thank him. He looked at me for a second then proceeded up the last few stairs.

When we reached the door he froze. His body stiffened and his nostrils flared. I frowned, turning to unlock the door when he grabbed my wrist, pulling me behind him, his body acting like an iron shield. The next thing I knew the door flew open as Erin stood in the opening in her pink sweatpants and matching tank top, almost crouched like she were ready for a fight. Her curly blonde hair was brightened by the unusual color of her now shimmering turquoise eyes which were rounded like my attacker's had been. Morgan's lips pulled back over his lips as he let out a low hiss. They stared at each other for a few long moments before Morgan finally broke the tense silence.

"What are you doing here feline?" he asked in a low and even voice.

Erin didn't move from her defensive stance as she answered, the words flowing out in a growl, "I live here you lifeless, walking sack of bones. What are *you* doing here?" Peeking around Morgan's arm I didn't recognize the intimidating person occupying the space in the doorway. I'd never heard her say anything mean before.

Morgan turned to me, "Do you know who this is?" he asked, his eyes gentle. I heard Erin gasp as she finally saw me standing behind him.

I nodded. His face lit up with surprise and comprehension.

"If you've hurt her in any way, consider yourself dead," she grunted, "well more dead than you are now."

Still looking at me, his lips curled up into a mischievous smile. "I thought you smelled different, like a mountain lion but with something sweeter, very pleasant in fact, I just couldn't figure out why. I was wondering why you'd want to associate with the furry kind."

He said the last word while turning to stare back at Erin. I sat there stunned, utterly confused, feeling overloaded by this night that seemed to stretch on relentlessly with surprises.

She snorted, "At least I don't suck the life out of living things, vampire." His eyes tightened as his smile faded.

I frowned before my eyes began to widen as I absorbed what she'd said.

"Vampire?" I breathed, the word feeling oddly familiar as it passed through my lips.

He stared at me with a sober expression and his jaw clenched tight.

I shifted my eyes to Erin, "Mountain lion?" She gazed back at me with unease dancing in her eyes. We all stood there, frozen in different positions of uncertainty.

"Well, that explains a lot." I muttered, my eyebrows raised thinking of all the odd things I'd noticed about him and her. I stood there appraising him, realizing that he was more beautiful than how any of my books had ever described his kind.

His dark eyes found mine as he took a step forward. "You're not afraid, not terrified that you're in the presence of two dangerous creatures that hunger for your blood and could quite literally kill you in an instant?"

I shuddered inwardly and then shrugged. "After what I've been through tonight? You saved me and she's my best friend, neither of you have tried to kill me so far." I looked from him to her and back again. "I have questions though, lots of questions, like what were you and Madelyn trying to do to me in the hospital, what's with the electric current I feel whenever you touch me, who are Kyle and Mitch? I'm guessing Madelyn and Dr. Blake are...vampires too?"

Erin spoke before he could. "Electric current? What's she talking about?"

Morgan sighed. Looking at me he said, "For one, not killing you has been..." his lips moved around as he searched for the correct word, "difficult. Two, yes Dr. Blake is a vampire and no, Madelyn isn't. She's something entirely different." He glanced back at Erin and, motioning to me, said, "She has magic in her blood, we don't know what kind, but I imagine that's what makes her smell so sweet. As for the current, I'm not sure."

This time Erin's face lit with understanding. "That's why every guy at this school likes you, the magic."

I blinked, looking at her, baffled.

Morgan ran his fingers through his hair again. "It's late. She's got a test in the morning and needs her rest." He gently took my chin in his cold, smooth hand, pulling my face around to look at him. I'd still been gaping at Erin's last comment.

"I will explain everything in time, but you need to sleep." I started to object, wanting to solve all of the night's mysteries, but he had put his finger across my lips, shaking his head.

"I'll be here in the morning and we will discuss this with Blake tomorrow. There's no turning back now anyway, unfortunately," he finished, his tone sounding morose.

He was right, I did have a test in the morning and I could feel the edges of sleep pulling at my consciousness. I was exhausted.

He paused, looking at me with wary eyes before leaning slowly, cautiously forward to place his cool lips against my cheek. He breathed in as my heart began to race before he leaned away, his deep blue eyes locked on mine. I could feel warmth flood my cheeks as I smiled up at him.

"Tomorrow then," I mumbled dazed, nodding as I turned to stumble past Erin who was rolling her eyes and shaking her head slowly from side to side.

"Give me a little warning next time vampire, you almost got eaten," Erin griped.

He raised an eyebrow.

"Sure thing fur ball." He winked at me, flashing his brilliant smile before turning to leave. She practically slammed the door shut behind him, an exasperated look on her face.

I plopped down on the edge of the couch in the small sitting room my head fuzzy, the cool softness of his lips still lingering on my cheek. Erin lay down across from me on the other couch propped up on one elbow on her side. I felt like a child learning that Santa Clause, or in this case the monster under your bed, really in fact did exist. As I sat there trying to work the puzzle out in my head I decided there were a few things that I was sure about. My best friend was a mountain lion, the only guy I've really ever been interested in was a vampire, and I'm different...whatever that means.

Erin was grinning at me. "So, that's the guy you were talking about the other day?" she teased then shrugged, "Not my type, of course, but to each her own." We sat there a moment before a frown formed on her face, her eyes focusing on the bruises on my neck.

"What happened to you Ansley?"

I was still lost, digesting everything. I looked at the person sitting across from me; the person who I thought was silly and messy with a life that revolved purely around guys. What little did I know. She waited patiently, quietly stroking Webster's head who was curled up, purring next to her.

I blew out a puff of air and explained, "I was walking home from the library when something threw me into a tree and tried to choke me to death. How long have you been a...mountain lion?" As tired as I was, I didn't think I would be able to actually sleep, so I was hoping Erin would be more forthcoming with answers than Morgan, who'd done nothing but avoid everything.

"Thing, what thing?"

I shifted restlessly, "I don't know, I thought he was just some guy then his whole body started to tremble and his eyes. Do your eyes ever change to a pale gold..."

I trailed off as I caught a glimpse of her expression. She was motionless, shock frozen on her face.

"Erin?" I leaned forward on the edge of the couch, anxious, preparing to heave myself over to her, but she reacted first. She sprung from her couch, rushing over to put her arms around me in a hug.

"Ansley, I'm so glad you're okay. Do you know how lucky you are?"

I hugged her back, slightly confused.

"He was a werewolf, probably one of the ones we've been looking for," she gushed. "We don't know which one killed the girl the other night, that's why we had to attend a council meeting this weekend." She paused and sniffed. "Hey, you do smell good."

I stiffened, suddenly aware that Erin was probably extremely dangerous, even if she was my best friend.

She leaned back shaking with laughter. "Just kidding Ansley. There is something different about you though. I can't believe I didn't see it or smell it for that matter." She appraised me, still smiling.

I shook my head, trying to figure out what to say. I stood and started to pace.

"Hold on, council meeting, what council meeting? Who's the 'we' and there's more than one? I thought you were with Scott this weekend. Why won't you tell me how long you've been a mountain lion? Please, don't tell me you're dodging my questions too." I groaned at the end, continuing to pace with my arms folded across my chest.

She sighed, "I guess you'll figure this all out eventually, so I might as well tell you." She watched me pace for a moment, hesitating. "There was a council meeting this weekend because of the murder the other night to decide how we were going to capture and punish the werewolf that did it, and to figure out why he or she did it. The 'we' is Scott and me."

I stopped pacing, gaping at her as I grasped this new piece of information.

"Yes, Scott is a lion too and I'm not dodging your question. I've been one ever since I turned thirteen, when I hit puberty of course. Both my parents were lions so naturally I am too. Some of the myths about us are true, others are just crap. For one, we aren't crazy beasts like werewolves and we don't change form when a full moon is out. We can shift anytime we want. And no, anger doesn't trigger the change, nor does any other surge of emotion. It's completely under our control. We do have a few other powers like a ridiculously awesome sense of smell, extraordinary hearing, we're extremely fast, and very strong. But we're pretty much like everybody else on this earth, just trying to live life and be happy. The only drawback is that like most other shapeshifters, we do crave blood and we can be dangerous." Smirking she added, "So, the bone bag won't come clean about himself, huh?"

I had sunken down onto the couch while she'd been spouting the life and times of a mountain lion. I shrugged, my shoulders hunched with all the newly learned details weighing me down. This was nothing like I'd read in my books.

"Something like that," I mumbled then frowned. "Hey what about your eyes, they change right?"

"Yeah, to whatever color we have an affinity for, mine turn turquoise."

We sat there for a few more quiet moments before she looked at me, her face serious. "I'd like to be able to tell you about that lifeless thing you're interested in, but we're bound by the B.E.R.E not to share each other's secrets, only he can tell you about himself and his kind's vile nature. Just don't be fooled, he and his kind are just as dangerous and unpredictable as we are." _Danger._ I never thought my life would be filled with so much so quickly.

"B.E.R.E?"

"Yeah, the Book of Exceptional Rarities of Earth. It outlines all the rules and such for all supernatural beings. It's a lot of complicated blah if you ask me, but whatever, I still have to follow it."

"Huh." There was a book for everything apparently.

"Hey, just do me a favor and be careful around that leech," she said looking at me intently. I nodded. I still didn't feel like I'd asked everything I'd wanted, but I was having more and more trouble keeping my eyes open.

Erin made the decision for me. "You need a shower and sleep. You'll find your answers soon enough." She smiled, but her expression changed. Wary she asked, "Best friends?"

"Best friends," I said nodding and smiled, heaving myself up toward the stairs. I paused on the first step, turning toward her. "So, why do you keep it just above freezing in here?"

"My body temperature runs a bit higher than yours so I've got to have it cooler to stay comfortable and not over heat. I'd die if I lived anywhere there's any kind of long summer."

"Hmm. Makes sense, I guess." I paused for a second. "Then that's why you sleep so late? You're out prowling the night with Scott?"

I smirked as she grinned back. "Yeah, something like that."

"Just don't forget to wipe your paws," I added.

"Hardee-har, go shower. I think you're getting a little loopy," she said giggling.

"Probably."

I shuffled up the staircase and down the hall to the bathroom. I turned on the hot water, the steam fogging up the small space as I got undressed and removed the bandages from my hands. The cuts were puffy and red, but not bleeding anymore. I let the water slowly wash away all the tension from the evening, trying to keep as much of it off my hands as possible because it stung. I threw on my night clothes, re-bandaged my hands, brushed my teeth and hair and headed for my inviting bed. It was past three before I fell into a sleep that was full of nightmares.

Chapter 4: Instincts

∽

I opened my eyes the next morning to a light streaming through the window that threw a pale yellow glow throughout the room. Everything felt bright, worry free as if nothing had ever happened. I glanced down the length of the bed to see Webster curled in a tight ball at my feet. Everything seemed absolutely normal.

Until I made the mistake of stretching. My entire body ached with a stiffness that felt like I'd run head on into a brick wall. As I swallowed, the thick dryness in my throat caused the previous night to slam into me, knocking the air from my chest as all of its realizations collided with my consciousness. My hands felt chapped under the bandages. I suddenly felt exhausted. I pulled the pillow over my face just before my alarm clock began its annoyingly loud beep. It was inevitable, I had to get up. I had to take a test today and I wanted to see Morgan.

I headed for the bathroom to begin my morning routine of waking up. I flicked the light on and stared at the person in the mirror. The dark circles under my eyes starkly contrasted with my skin that was even paler than usual. I leaned in closer examining the dark bruises around my neck in the shape of a perfect handprint that almost looked painted on. I let out a deflated sigh before beginning to work the knots out of my hair. After adding a little make up in an attempt to give my face a little color, pulling the bandages off my hands, and brushing my teeth I left the bathroom and headed for my closet.

I hunted through the small space for something to wear. I settled on a pair of faded jeans and a long sleeve gray turtleneck that fit snuggly. I threw on my leather jacket and black boots, checked that my can of pepper spray was safely tucked inside my bag, and that my wallet was in my back pocket. I bounded down the stairs and out the front door ready for the long day ahead of me.

I jumped, letting out a yelp when I found Morgan leaning against the wall next to the door. His arms crossed, head down, motionless in his state of thought. I watched as the statue slowly came alive as he turned his head and smiled.

"Good morning," he murmured as I attempted to slow my breathing and my heart.

"Hi," I breathed, smiling in return.

"How was the rest of your evening?" His face seemed amused like he knew something I didn't.

"Restless," I sighed. He nodded as he pushed off the wall.

"And yours?" We started down the steps, heading for his shiny black car. The few strands of dark hair that shadowed his forehead moved slightly as we walked. His lips were still curved up in a smile.

"Uneventful," he answered.

"So, what exam are we taking today?" he added, his tone light and comfortable.

I grunted, "It's not like you don't already know, considering that you've probably memorized my entire schedule and work hours."

He chuckled quietly. "True. It is important to know where the person you are following...protecting, I guess is a better word now, going to be. I may have to make it a full time hobby."

My stomach proceeded to do cartwheels as I fumbled for something to say, the silence growing. I wanted to ask him again why he was following me. But I opted for something off subject. I didn't want another answer like what I'd gotten last night and part of me was oddly happy that he was.

"How old are you?" I blurted, the surge of questions I'd had pent up last night flooding back.

"I'm eighteen. And yourself?" he asked as he opened the passenger door for me, shutting it and getting in on the other side before I had time to answer. We headed toward the college with a swiftness that made me glance out the window nervously for cops.

"Same." I hesitated as we pulled into the main campus parking lot. He smoothly stopped the car in the space next to my old red jeep. The crisp air nipped at my cheeks as he opened my door. "H-how old are you, really?" I stammered.

He smiled wryly, "You mean how long have I been a vampire?"

I nodded, shifting my focus to the pavement as we headed toward the liberal arts building.

He sighed, the smile on his face fading slightly. "I was born into this life in 1896, so I'm guessing that would put me somewhere around one hundred and twelve or so. I forget sometimes."

I tried to hide my shock, smiling at two students as they passed by us, their eyes locked on the vampire next to me.

He saw right through my weak attempt. "Surprised? I'm betting you thought I was thousands of years old, seen the societies of ancient times rise and fall." He finished with a condescending smile pasted on his lovely face.

He leaned closely as we kept walking, his voice almost a whisper, "There are a lot of fallacies in the stories that are told about my kind, don't believe everything you read." Feeling his cool breath tickle my neck, I shuddered.

He leaned away, clenching his teeth. I looked up at him to see his dark blue eyes focused on the sidewalk.

"I wonder why your eyes are such a dark blue...I mean, I've never seen eyes your color before," I said. He blinked, looking away. I watched as he grimaced, conflict etched on his features.

"I'm sorry. I didn't mean to offend you."

He looked down at me then, a stunned look on his face. "You haven't offended me. This is just," he paused, "difficult. I've shared my reasons for existence with only one other and now they no longer live. I never thought I'd be sharing my life again. And here you are taking all of this so calmly, talking to me as if I were any normal person." He inhaled deeply, "You *are* different, more than I even expected."

This time I was the one to look away, letting my dark curtain of hair slide around my shoulder between us.

We walked a few more steps. "The simple version is that they changed when I was changed," he explained casually.

I tucked my hair behind my ear. "And the not simple version?"

His intense eyes caught mine, "I'll explain that one later."

"And the light? I thought you could only be out at night?"

He chuckled lightly, a soft rumble. "Myth," he said, shaking his head. "Like I said, you can't believe everything you read. Granted bright sunlight is uncomfortable for my eyes, much like looking into direct sunlight would be for a human, but no, I'm not going to burst into flame."

We were walking up the steps to the liberal arts building when he stepped in front of me and pulled the door open, waiting for me to walk through.

"I believe we have a test to take," he said smiling. I didn't want to take a test right now. It seemed so small compared to all the questions bouncing around in my head. How was I supposed to concentrate with my head filled with thoughts of mountain lions, vampires, and werewolves?

As he opened the classroom door, the dull hum of voices greeted us. We headed to the very top row of seats. He leaned in, his cool breath tickling my ear as he whispered, "Don't worry. You're going to do fine."

I turned my head to find his face inches from mine, a wide smile stretched across his smooth skin. "Can you read my mind now too?" I tripped on a step because my eyes had been focused on him and not where I was going. He caught me by my waist gracefully, never missing a beat.

"If only. I pick up senses, feelings, I guess you could say. It's part of being what I am; you know when your prey is afraid. Call it predatory instincts." He shrugged. "Right now, you're tense. I'm assuming it's because of this test that you haven't spent enough time cramming for."

Tense was an understatement. My nerves were tighter than piano wire. I slid into my seat as he glided into his next to me. I pulled out my notebook and tapped my pencil against the desk nervously.

Morgan watched me, humor on his face. "Would you like me to distract you?"

I looked over at him as he closed one eye in a wink.

I resisted the urge to stick my tongue out at him. "You're doing a fine job already," I grumbled.

Professor Fowler cleared his throat at the front of the room, the buzz of voices around us slacking to silence. He was like any other middle-aged professor, thick black rimmed glasses and dressed head to toe in tweed. He had begun explaining the rules for the exam, but I was already lost in the dull hum of energy vibrating in the space between Morgan and me. I turned my head to see him tense. His eyes shifted to mine.

"Can you feel that?" I whispered.

He nodded stiffly, turning his attention back forward. Professor Fowler had started to hand out the test. I quickly cleared my desk of my notebook before he handed me the thick paper booklet. I took a deep breath and curled my fingers into a fist in an attempt to concentrate as I read through the first question. I started to scribble out my answer when the lead on my pencil broke from all the pressure I was putting on it. I sighed and began fumbling through my bag for a pen when I saw a white hand flash beside me and turned to see a simple black pen sitting harmlessly on my desk. I stared at him amazed. He smiled at me impishly before looking back down at his test.

Of course, he finished before me and walked smoothly to the front of the room to hand in his exam and then out the door. He paused to smile wryly before quietly disappearing. I spent the next twenty minutes writing the answers to the last few essay questions, the pen racing across the paper furiously. I nearly ran down the steps to turn it in. Professor Fowler glanced up from his book briefly to offer a small smile. I returned the gesture and headed for the door.

Morgan was standing exactly where I expected him to. He was leaning next to the door in the same casual position I'd found him this morning, his eyes focused as he stood there thinking. He lifted his head, turning his deep blue eyes on me.

"How was it?"

"You were there, you took it, you should know."

He grinned. "Yes, but I'm not worried whether I pass or fail."

I grimaced, stupid heightened vampire senses. "Who said I was worried?" I said miffed.

"You didn't have to," he replied as he reached over to lightly tap his finger on my forehead, the cool sensation increasing the electric hum between us.

He withdrew his hand, jaw tightening as he looked away.

We started for the doors. It was past eleven and I realized I hadn't had any breakfast during my rush to see Morgan this morning. My stomach grumbled in confirmation. Although I wanted to eat, I wanted to get the meeting with Dr. Blake over with more. As Morgan opened the door for me I walked past him and headed for the registration building. I felt him grab the back of my jacket and yank me back.

"Where do you think you're going?"

"To see Dr. Blake," I replied, leaning away from him.

"Oh no, not until you've got some food in your stomach, I know you have to eat more frequently, being human."

"Can't we see him first?" I insisted attempting to pull free of his iron grasp.

"Actually, he's out of town for the day."

I scowled at him but quit pulling away. "And when were you planning on telling me?"

He grinned, "About ten seconds ago."

"Fine," I said as I turned in the opposite direction toward the commons. He caught up with me easily, matching my pace.

"Something on your mind Ansley?" he asked softly.

"I've got a lot of things on my mind, especially since the last day or so if you hadn't noticed, since you seem to catch on to everything else so quickly." I let the words spout out freely as I glared at the concrete, the trees, everything but his beautiful face that was shadowed by his dark hair, his pristine, soft lips, and his fierce blue eyes.

"Will you have dinner with me in a couple of weeks, Saturday night?" The question surprised me. I stopped walking and spun to look at him.

"What? Why?"

"To eat of course," he paused, "it would also give me the opportunity to tell you about myself, to eliminate a few of those overly imaginative myths you have floating around in your head. Besides, midterms will be over so you won't have to worry about studying."

He took a step closer so that his face was just inches from mine. "Plus, you're in my life now...and I don't think I want that to change," he breathed. I felt his cool breath on my face as his dark eyes held mine.

I swallowed, trying to keep my breathing even so I wouldn't hyperventilate as my heart tried to beat its way out of my chest.

I wanted to close the gap between us I could feel the electricity tingling in the air in the small space. I settled for a nod and said, "Sure."

He smiled and leaned away, turning to walk again. This time I matched his pace, dizzy as we quietly entered the commons.

Surprisingly, it wasn't as busy today as it had been yesterday. Once we filled our trays full of food, he led the way to a table by the window in a far corner of the large cafeteria. I hungrily bit took a bite of my club sandwich. Morgan watched me carefully as he pushed around his mound of mashed potatoes with his fork. I was surprised he'd gotten anything at all. I didn't think vampires could eat real food.

"How long have you lived in Corvallis?" he asked, still playing with his pile of mush.

I swallowed and took a swig of my soda. "Since I started school, you?"

Instead of answering he asked, "What are your parents like?"

"My mother is a high school literature teacher who is scatterbrained but still sort of obsessive compulsive about everything and my father is an accountant for a large bank. He's easy going compared to her. Why?"

He shook his head, stabbing little individual peas with his fork, "Why do you read so much? What are your other interests?"

"I like reading. No matter how complex, everything in books seems less complicated than real life. I don't know, I like a lot of things." I frowned. "What's with the twenty questions routine and how did you know I like to read a lot?"

Again with the shrugging. I scowled at him, leaning back in my chair and crossing my arms, refusing to give him any more information about myself.

His eyes narrowed as he leaned back in his chair, mirroring my challenging attitude. "Curiosity, you could say."

"How long have you been following me anyway?"

"Long enough to know things about you that you don't even know about yourself."

"Are you trying to scare me?"

"Hardly," he said, "More like slowly pushing you into a realization of what your life really is."

Okay, now I was confused. "You lost me."

"I'm sure, but that's okay for now."

I looked out the window, searching for the meaning of what he was trying to say. I replayed his different facial expressions, all the off-handed comments he pushed into our conversations. I watched him curiously, waiting for him to put the growing load of peas into his mouth. He looked at me then, a crooked smile forming on his face as he slid the stuffed fork into his mouth and chewed. I managed to keep my mouth from dropping open.

"I thought you couldn't eat food." I said dumbfounded.

He shrugged. "Myth." He swallowed and gently laid the fork down on his tray.

"What do you like reading?" he asked.

"I don't know, vampires, werewolves, stuff like that."

His eyebrows rose slightly. "That's a little coincidental."

"What?"

"Vampires and werewolves."

"Okay."

"Why do you think it is that you're interested in such supernatural things, that you've spent so much time submerging yourself in a place where such things could be true? Why did you choose a school where the Dean is a vampire? More importantly, I don't think many people have a mountain lion for a roommate. You're surrounded by so many creatures you never thought existed." I looked at him, surprised he'd just said so much.

"I chose this school because it was away from every-one I knew. So I could have a fresh start where no one knew me." I said. It was just an excuse though. I was feeling more and more like I was here for a reason. He'd made his point. It was uncanny how deeply I was already involved with the supernatural side of things.

"Who knows." I added and grimaced remembering Madelyn's comment that I was different. We sat there for a few moments in silence.

"Any more exams today?"

I snorted. "You should know."

He grinned. "And of course, I do."

We'd finished eating. Well I'd finished, he more or less had made a display of appearing to eat. Even though he made a good show of it, I didn't think he really liked food.

We made our way toward the parking lot. I could feel my steps becoming smaller and slower as I tried to make the walk last as long as possible. I waited for him to say something, but he just quietly matched my ever slowing pace. I took a deep breath enjoying the moment, feeling for once calm and at ease in the company of another.

His smooth voice broke the soft beat of our walk. "What are you thinking?"

"No one is staring at me, glaring or anything. It's sort of ironic, but I feel normal."

He frowned. "Glaring?"

"Girls don't seem to like me, all except Erin of course and guys, well...they can't seem to not look at me like I'm some sort of thing that they've never seen before."

"Hmm...well I imagine no one is staring because of the magic."

I looked at him surprised. "So you do have powers."

He nodded. "Many. And so do you."

"So, you're saying that unknowingly I'm willing everyone that is around us right now to not look at us?" I asked sarcastically.

He chuckled. "No, that would be me. You do have powers though."

"What powers?" We stopped beside his car. He reached past me to open the passenger door. I made no move toward the dark opening as I sat there staring up into his dark blue eyes.

"How about we add this to the list of myths you have about vampires that we're going to discuss during our dinner date?"

"You're avoiding me again." I said, stepping closer to him.

"No, merely stalling."

"Same difference."

"Perhaps, but patience is a virtue."

"I'm not virtuous or patient."

He looked at me then, his deep blue eyes gazing at me from under dark lashes with an expression something like frustration. I could feel a static pressure slowly begin to slide up my arm.

"It's not going to work you know, the whole hypnotic thing." He blinked then, his eyes refocusing on my face.

"You have exams to worry about," he said finally with a sigh. What was he avoiding? I ground my teeth together in defeat. I knew he wouldn't tell me. Yet.

"Sure." I said deflated as I slid into the soft leather seat.

The ride was silent. I stole glances at him periodically as I tried to figure out different ways to get him to open up. I was sure he knew what I was thinking as he stared fixedly at the road. When we pulled in front of my house I finally broke the silence, "When is Dr. Blake going to be back?"

"Tomorrow," he paused, "can I drive you again?"

"I'd like that," I answered almost too quickly. "Since my jeep is still at school and all." I added coolly. I could feel my cheeks turning pink from embarrassment.

We settled back into our familiar silence as we walked up to the front door. He finally stopped and turned to me smiling, "Tomorrow then." He leaned down and gently pressed his lips against my cheek breathing in the same way he had the night before. I froze as the familiar feeling of my rapid heartbeat pushed my blood like liquid fire through my veins. I attempted to control my smile as he slowly leaned back to settle his dark eyes on me. I clumsily fished my keys out of my bag and unlocked the door. It was almost impossible to shut it as I watched him stroll down the steps to his car.

The night passed more sluggishly then I could have ever thought possible. Eventually, I gave up on studying and opted for a good book. My effort to lodge myself into the fantasy world was futile though. I tried more than one book but each time I'd read a few pages only to find one of the characters too much like Morgan. Most of them were vampires, of course. But, whether it was the dark hair or pale skin, I couldn't get my mind off his perfect lips and the way they stretched into that perfect smile.

I settled on lying in bed and looking at the clock every few minutes. I finally fell into sleep some time past one in the morning. I couldn't even escape him there as he played the main character in my dreams.

Chapter 5: Assumptions

⁓

When I woke the next morning, the sun was bright and shining. I ran through a shower and threw on clothes with a speed I never knew I had. Throughout the process I peeked out of the closest window to see if his sleek black car was sitting outside waiting. As I finished washing down a granola bar with milk I heard a light knock on the front door. I felt my nerves stretch even tighter.

I grasped the cool handle and opened the door slowly so I wouldn't seem as hyped up as I felt. He stood there in a dark blue New York baseball hat smiling the wry smile I'd dreamed about. Apparently, I hadn't fooled him. I half smiled back simultaneously attempting to stay calm and appear just as such. I failed miserably. I couldn't get over how perfectly the blue hat matched his eyes.

"How was your evening?" he asked mutedly.

"Long." To say the least. "I imagine yours passed pretty slowly too." I added quietly. Having lived over a century, he must be bored with a lot of things by now. He's probably tried every extreme sport or hobby that exists.

"Actually, I was quite busy for the most of the evening," he said frowning.

"Oh," I paused. "Doing what?" I blurted without thinking. Something I seemed to do often in his company.

"Hunting," he replied as we got in the car.

"Oh." There's something I'd forgotten to consider in my list of hobbies for the undead. Of course he had to do what vampires are known for at some point. The thought wasn't as scary as I'd figured it would be.

I felt all the tenseness I'd had last night and this morning dissolve as I watched the orange and red leaves slide past the window in a blur. This morning seemed better than any other October morning I'd experienced. The trees and the leaves couldn't have looked more beautiful. It was as if they'd been picked out of a painting and placed there.

As we sauntered up the path to the main building I couldn't keep myself from asking, "So, about the magic."

He sighed, smiling slightly, "You're relentless aren't you?" He opened the door for me and said, "Later."

We walked into the administrator's office and the same woman who helped me last time looked up from beside one of the filing cabinets. She tucked a folder into the opened drawer, closed it and walked over to the counter.

"What can I do for you?" She was looking at me, but Morgan was the one who answered.

"We're here to see Dr. Blake, if we could please," he answered quietly, his voice smooth as silk. She shifted her eyes from me to him, a smile widening on her face as she took in the sight of Morgan.

"Your name?" She pulled out her yellow sticky pad and pen, her eyes never leaving his.

"My name is Morgan and this is Ansley."

"That's right, I remember you." She finished writing our names and clicked the pen. "Have a seat. I'll let him know you're here."

She turned and disappeared through the heavy wooden door. Before we even sat down she reappeared.

"He's ready for you," she announced as she bustled us into his office and clicked the door shut.

Morgan led the short distance across the room to Dr. Blake's desk. He looked up from his scattered papers, smiling warmly as he laid his pen down. He seemed the same as he had the first time I'd come. Everything about him was perfect, right down to his flawless pale skin.

He stood, shaking Morgan's hand. "Morgan it's always a pleasure, I'm glad you were able stop by." He looked to me, "And how are you today Ansley?"

"Good," I stammered, mustering up a weak smile. He nodded in response. I was still trying to grasp the fact that I was standing in a room with two vampires.

"Have you learned anything new?" Morgan asked quietly. The two vampires exchanged wary glances at me before Dr. Blake heaved a sigh. Why did I suddenly feel like they both knew something they weren't telling me?

"Yes and I've made some rather interesting discoveries." He began shuffling through a cabinet behind his desk. He pulled out a manila folder and laid it on the stack of papers, placing his hands on top of it before looking across to me.

"Ansley, you do realize that from this point, everything you hear, see, and learn must be kept a secret." Like everything I'd already discovered wasn't some sort of confidential enigma already. Apparently things were just going to continue spiraling into the unreal. I could feel both of them eyeing me intently, waiting for my response. I nodded and felt Morgan relax next to me, the humming energy between us quieting the slightest bit. I hadn't noticed he was so tense until then.

Dr. Blake inhaled deeply as he opened the thin, cream colored folder. I could see a photograph and a few loose papers full of writing.

"This isn't easy to say and I'm sorry to have to be the one to tell you, but you were adopted." The words flowed over me as he continued, "By what Morgan has told me about you and the way you feel and smell I'm positive your real parents, well, at least one of them was elfin. I'm not sure who they were yet, but I'm still making phone calls and digging." He paused, turning his blue eyes up to look at me. I hadn't realized, but my fingers were gripping the arms of the chair as I tried to control my breathing. I felt like the air around me was trying to crush my suddenly hollow chest.

Morgan slowly reached over and put his hand on mine, the feel of his cool fingers held off the hyperventilation bubbling in my lungs.

"I'm truly sorry, but I think it's important for you to know. Do you want me to continue?" I couldn't keep from nodding as the vibration coming from Morgan kept everything at a dull haze.

Dr. Blake picked the picture up and placed it in front of me, "Do you know who this is?"

I looked down at the boyish face and familiar dark hair and muscular arms. "Chase?" I breathed, looking up at Dr. Blake. "What does he have to do with any of this?" I asked defensively, my voice low and firm. I didn't want the one person left that I knew was normal to be a part of this new crazy and unpredictable life.

He spoke slowly, "He is your guardian, so to speak."

"What do you mean?" I asked confused.

"I mean, he's here to watch over you, to be there for you whenever necessary. Your real parents arranged for him to be in your life, to be close by. Because of your lineage and the magic in your blood, the male population is naturally attracted to you. Therefore they cast a spell so that he'd only see you as a close friend." That explained a lot, no wonder we'd never dated.

"Whoever your parents are, they're powerful and by hiding you they very possibly have a number of enemies."

I was still processing the fact that my parents weren't my biological parents and that Chase was, well he was still Chase, I guess. Dr. Blake was still speaking but it was only a lifeless drone in the background of the thoughts roaring through my head. I could feel Morgan next to me, tense as he watched me begin to internally crumble, the energy coming from him starting to crackle like fire.

I stood numbly. Dr. Blake was still talking. I heard myself say, "I'll be right back, just have to go to the bathroom," but I felt detached from myself. Morgan's anxious gaze barely registered in my mind as I turned and walked out of the office.

I walked blindly down the quiet hall, opened the door to the cold, wet air, and stepped out in the direction of the many nature trails surrounding the campus. I didn't realize I'd started running until my face felt cool with sweat, my hair sticking to my head from the cold rain that had seeped through the trees to pelt the forest floor. I stopped, the air sweeping in and out of my lungs, burning as I tried to slow my breathing.

I looked around me, observing the heavy underbrush and large trees. I walked a few more steps before sinking down in the middle of the trail, the wet leaves soaking through my jeans. My life was a lie. Everything I knew was a mask, shadowing a truth that was purposefully kept from me. I'd always felt like I didn't fit in, at least now I had a reason. But who was I? I sat there trying to remember as much of my past as I could, holding onto the memories in hopes they'd crush this new information. But, Dr. Blake's words kept resurfacing, starting the process over again.

I eventually ended up just sitting there, listening to the quiet tap of the rain on the leaves and the ground, my mind sinking back into numbness. I hadn't realized the sun had started to set until my clothes were completely soaked and I started to shiver.

I heaved myself up slowly, stiff from sitting so long, my fingers and face slightly numb from the cold. I kept my eyes down following the path. The trees were now only shadows in the quickly fading glow of the day. The rain continued as I pushed my heavy legs faster, ready to be out of the suddenly eerie woods and my wet clothes.

I'd been wondering how far I'd gone when a large gray wolf suddenly stepped out from the thick brush beside the trail. Only thing was—it didn't look like any wolf I'd ever seen. Its mouth was huge displaying a set of perfect white teeth with an overly long one hanging on either side that resembled something akin to tusks. Its ears were larger and furry and it had what looked like a thick, coarse mane that wrapped around its neck and traveled down its chest. Its front two legs seemed normal, but the back two were warped with bulky muscles. I froze as my gut tightened with fear. My mind dredged up the comment Dr. Blake made about enemies and the werewolf that Erin had said I'd been so lucky to have dodged. The wolf's shimmering slate gray eyes focused on me as it slowly crept toward me flashing its sharp teeth.

"Wait, I'm not who you think I am." I spoke quickly, trying to play dumb and stall as I stumbled back a step. The wolf blinked, pausing for a second evaluating me with its eyes. Maybe it was considering what I was saying. Maybe it would turn around and I could run back to my jeep, vowing to never walk in the woods alone again. Maybe not. It took another step in my direction. A flash of light ahead flickered through the trees onto the trail. The wolf looked over its shoulder before turning to take another step toward me. The light became brighter, sweeping back and forth. If I let out a scream maybe it would run off. I took a deep breath when it stopped, seeming to let out a sigh before it disappeared into the thick brush. I was suddenly racing toward the light when I heard someone call my name.

"Ansley?" The warm rumble sounded familiar.

I stopped, forcing my eyes to focus on who was coming toward me.

"Ansley, is that you?" Chase asked anxiously as he finished the last few yards in a slow jog, the light now bouncing up and down.

"Are you okay? Geez Ansley, I've been looking for you for hours." He wrapped his arms around me in a hug. He felt warm, like the home that I knew, smelling of clean soap and rain. I shivered, reminded of how cold I was.

"You must be freezing!" He shrugged off his coat and wrapped it around me, I started to explain that it was pointless, but he kept talking.

"What are you doing out here? You're soaked." He stuck the flashlight in his back pocket before he wrapped his arm around my shoulders, leading us into the direction he had come from. I didn't reply, so he continued to talk.

"Strange, but I was in my room on my computer when I heard a light knock on my door. When I opened it no one was there except an envelope with your keys in it and a piece of paper taped to the door that said you were somewhere in the woods and needed help. It was signed with an M. Who's M?" It figured he would send someone to come find me after I disappeared the way I did. I felt drained from everything, a piece of me wondering why he didn't come himself.

I shrugged. Aside from walking, talking seemed like a task that was too much for me right now. We were coming to an opening in the woods, it was almost completely dark. We stopped at the first building, ducking under the waterfall of rain from the overhang to stand under the little space that was protected from the heavy downpour.

His arm slid down to my elbow, pulling me around to stare into his brown eyes.

"Come on Ansley, talk to me. What's bothering you?" Chase's eyes searched mine, as if he could pull the answer from them.

I looked at the human being in front of me. The one person who seemed untouched in this newly discovered life. He wasn't a werewolf or a vampire, he was just Chase. Sure there was the magic influencing our relationship, but *he* seemed normal. I wanted to tell him about the wolf, about everything, wanted to cry into his shoulder while he told some funny story that made everything seem less painful, less serious. But, I couldn't. I couldn't drag him into my frightening new reality any more than he already was and I wasn't entirely sure how much he knew, if anything.

"I think I failed my trig test and literature didn't look so great either," I lied, horribly.

He saw right through it. "Uh-huh, so you decided a long walk in the freezing rain until dark would be a great idea." His hand slid down to mine, he frowned as he felt the rough surface.

He turned it over, examining the shallow cuts, "What happened?"

"I tripped and fell last night, coming down the concrete steps in front of the library, wasn't paying attention. You know how I am sometimes."

I tried to sound nonchalant, hoping he would let it go. I relaxed when he looked back at me, grinning,

"Do you need me to walk you to your jeep every night?"

I was beginning to feel better, like the afternoon had never happened. His company was like a soft, warm blanket.

"As long as your girlfriends don't mind."

He chuckled, "*They* won't."

"Come on, we need to get you somewhere warm and into some dry clothes."

Even though the rain had slowed to a foggy mist, we practically ran the rest of the way to my jeep. His pace looked like an easy lope while I felt like a crippled animal sprinting next to him in an attempt to keep up.

We slowed once we reached the parking lot, easing to a stop at my jeep. Chase pulled my keys out of his pocket and handed them to me.

"I'd drive you home too, but I've got to finish some work on my computer. You sure you're okay, I'm not going to have to send out a search and rescue to the jungle?" he asked grinning.

I smiled. "I'm sure. Thanks Chase, sometimes I don't know what I'd do without you."

His grin widened and he winked. "Same here sunshine." I started to climb in the jeep as he turned to leave.

"Hey." He turned and put his hand on the door before I could close it. "I just want you to know that you can come to me for anything. I know there's more bothering you than you're letting on and even if you don't tell me what it is, I'm still here for you, no matter what. K?"

I nodded and said, "K," trying to hold back the tears threatening to brim over as he turned to leave.

The door groaned as I pulled it shut. I could barely see past the blur of tears by the time I reached the parking lot exit. It wasn't fair for him to feel like he had to protect me, I thought angrily. I realized I was going to have to find a way to release him from the magic. I would ask Morgan tomorrow in class. Maybe he would know who to talk to.

When I got home I walked sluggishly towards the house. I barely noticed my bag sitting next to the door. At least Morgan had remembered my bag. I thought sarcastically to myself. I can't believe I'd forgotten the darn thing.

The rest of the night was a quiet daze. Erin was in class, so I took my time in the shower, letting the hot water soak through my stiff bones. I brushed my hair and climbed into bed feeling completely and utterly wasted. I was ready for the day to be over, but sleep wasn't ready for me. I tossed and turned, unable to get comfortable as the blaring buzz of questions raced through my mind. Why would my parents get rid of me? What danger could be so bad that they couldn't protect me? Why didn't Morgan come to find me, why couldn't I stop thinking about him, why was there so much invisible energy when he was around, and why was I craving it now? I finally fell asleep, my dreams merely a replay of the long day.

Chapter 6:
Myth

∽

I walked into my history class a few minutes before it was supposed to start and went through my usual routine of heading for the top, back row. I pulled out my notebook and waited for class to begin, watching Dr. Hartley as he thumbed through his history book making the few final tweaks on the day's lesson plan. The minutes passed by as I waited for Morgan to slide into the seat next to me. I began drumming my fingers on the desk, the beat sharp, anxious. When class started and he still hadn't shown, my stomach started to tighten. Where was he? I felt like I'd done something wrong, like I was the reason he wasn't here. The hour ticked by slower than I ever thought possible.

When I went to grab lunch, I searched the cafeteria for him, my eyes constantly scanning the students as I gulped down my chicken and macaroni and cheese. By the time I got to trigonometry, I was desperately hoping he'd be there waiting for me in the high, far off row. When class was over I wanted him to be outside the door, casually leaning against the wall to explain that he'd had errands to run this morning. He wasn't there, vampires don't have errands.

When I got home, deflated from the day, I collapsed on my bed and let sleep wash over me. I woke in time to hurry off to work, remembering to stuff my pepper spray in my bag. My shift at the library passed just as slow as my day had. Every time I heard the heavy glass door sweep open my head reflexively snapped up hoping he'd be there smiling with his dark eyes, his tousled hair, and stunning smile. He never showed.

When my shift was over I really wanted to call Chase to ask him to walk me to my jeep again. But, in the end I decided not to because it didn't seem fair that I should call on someone who was only there because of some spell. I took a deep breath to steel my resolve, pulled out my pepper spray, and headed for the parking lot.

The sky was cloudless, full of stars, and a full moon. It was silent besides the click of my boots against the pavement. I kept my pace quick, my eyes constantly darting around me. By the time I reached the brightly lit area I was nearly out of breath, but in one piece. I enjoyed the short-lived feeling of accomplishment as I climbed in and listened to my jeep rumble with life.

The rest of the week continued on in the same fashion. Thursday, I woke up, and went to class. When I got home I wanted nothing more than to sneak off to my room and close the curtains before wrapping myself in my covers, but Erin had a different plan.

"Come on Ansley, it'll be fun," she said while leaning against my doorframe, her fingers clasped together in front of her face. She looked at me with her lips puckered into a pout.

I blew out a puff of air, "Sure, why not."

"You'll see, by the time you get your first strike you'll be feeling better," she said happily.

I looked out the window of her Volkswagen bug as we headed to Dead Wood, the local bowling alley. I didn't want to be around anyone tonight, didn't have the energy to deal with the looks and whispers.

She nudged me with her elbow, "Hey, I'm looking out for ya. Nobody's going to act strange tonight. Besides I've got some pretty sharp teeth. I could definitely give them something to talk about...or scream." I smiled, she knew me all too well.

There weren't many people, just a small group huddled around one of the pool tables and another bunch playing on one of the far lanes. We got our shoes and picked the lane on the opposite end of everyone. I was on my second turn trying to bowl another strike when Erin decided to start with the questions. She was even more inquisitive than Chase.

"So what happened, do I need to dismember him?" she asked politely.

"No, it's not him, it's me." I threw the ball with as much force as I could down the lane. It landed in the gutter.

"Okay, so I'm listening." She stood and picked up the ball she was using. I wanted to tell her, needed to, but it felt like if I said the words out loud it would only confirm everything. It would only make it more real. What the hell.

"I'm adopted and Chase is only my friend because some kind of magic was put on him so that he would protect me." I didn't feel like telling her that I was half-elf yet; maybe some other day when I felt more into the idea.

"I'm sure he'd be your friend anyway, you can't look at it that way hun. Do you know who your biological parents are?"

"No."

"We could do some research and find out."

"No, it's okay for now."

"What about Morgan, I haven't seen or smelled him lately," she said her top lip curling up slightly in disgust.

"I don't know, I think I may have freaked him out or something. Maybe he's mad at me."

"Mad at you, nah there's no way."

"Can we talk about something else?" I didn't want to think about him right now. I felt like I spent so much time thinking about someone who wasn't there. I needed to save that for when I went to bed and couldn't sleep again.

"Sure," she paused, "I think I'm in love with Scott."

"No kidding...really?" Erin, the flirt was in love. I think that's a first. I mustered up a smile. I was happy for her even if I felt like the most alone person in the world. We spent the rest of the evening talking about him and her and their relationship. I listened attentively, focusing so I wouldn't be thinking about anything else.

By Friday, I began to lose hope that Morgan was ever going to show up in my life again. Everything seemed to be falling back into its normal rhythm and it was a feeling I didn't like. I felt alone and missed him. I woke and followed my familiar routine of class and work. When I got home and reached the top of the stairs, glad that the day was over, I opened my door and set my bag on the desk. I laid my wallet down next to it glimpsing a small white square out of the corner of my eye. A delicate piece of paper folded in half laid carelessly on my bed. I picked it up, opening the thin sheet and read the elegant handwriting.

I was hoping our dinner plans were still intact, and therefore wanted to send you a reminder in case you'd forgotten. I will be at your door tomorrow evening at 7:00pm sharp.

M.

I slumped down on the bed, reading the short note over again. My heart fluttered at the thought that he hadn't disappeared and that I was going to see him again, soon. Had he been in my room or had he given the note to Erin to give to me? I thought vampires couldn't come in without being invited. I would have to ask her when she got in.

Oddly enough, at that moment I heard the front door open. Even from my room I could hear the bags of plastic crinkling together as she struggled to close the door and make her way up the stairs.

"Shopping again, huh?" I called out as she passed by my room.

"Yeah, they had some awesome sales at the mall today. I wish you could've come."

She heaved the bundles on my bed and began pulling out clothes piece by piece, showing them to me. I oo'd and aww'd at the appropriate times, my mind straying to the soft piece of paper in my hand.

"Maybe next time," I said when all the bags were finally empty. She continued to rummage through everything, pulling off tags and stickers.

"Hey, did you leave this here?" I held up the innocent piece of paper to her.

She frowned, reading the elegant writing I'd practically memorized.

"Huh. I thought I smelled something stale when I walked in; figured it was just his scent lingering from the other night. I'm going to have a chat with that vampire about staying out when we're not here."

I suddenly felt self conscious, wondering what he might have seen, if he might have looked through anything. At least my bedroom was neat and orderly, I always made the bed. My mother always said the bed was the focal point of the bedroom, if it was a mess, then the room was a mess. This thought only spurred what I'd learned a few days ago, causing my mood to sink. What was my real mother like and what were her thoughts on the appearance of a bed and its impact on a room? It sounded silly, but it hurt not knowing.

I slinked off to the bathroom to do my nightly routine before bed, feeling glum. When I came out Erin had migrated to her room and was still admiring her cotton trophies. I crawled under my covers after mumbling a good night. I slept and dreamed of a woman with long dark hair and bright green eyes. She was a mirror image of me.

I was grateful it was Saturday. I lay in bed happy that I didn't have to work and even more glad that I didn't have class. When I finally pulled myself from under the warm blankets the sun was bright and high in the sky. My alarm clock's blue glowing numbers told me that it was after eleven. It was the latest I'd slept in a while and it felt good.

After seeing everything Erin had brought home last night, I decided I needed to get out and buy something new to wear for tonight. Shopping usually cheered me up; I was after all a girl.

I gulped down a bowl of cereal before jumping in for a quick shower, brushing my teeth and hair, and throwing on a little concealer and blush. I could already feel myself getting nervous about tonight as I flitted around. I felt wired. I decided to blow dry my hair straight because it usually relaxed me. I felt calm until little flickers of Morgan would pop into my head, his smooth face, his smile, and his dark eyes. Inevitably, I found myself at square one again bustling around the little room, anxious. I patted Webster on the head before leaving, my spirits already feeling better from my excitement.

It was Saturday, so the mall was pretty busy. I managed my way through the crowds and made out with a hunter green, long sleeved sweater and a new pair of fashionably faded jeans. I loved jeans and never seemed to have enough. After grabbing a quick lunch in the courtyard I headed home. Shopping had done the trick. When I reached my room, I hung my new clothes, and curled up on my bed to read a little more of _The Picture of Dorian Gray_. I was finally in the mood to read again.

When the sun started to set, I knew I had about an hour to get ready. I laid my book on my nightstand, stretched, and headed to the bathroom. I brushed my teeth furiously, combed my hair, and reapplied my make up, making my eyes darker for the evening. The new shade brought out my brilliant green eyes.

I was anxious and excited, my nerves stretched tight. Once I'd dressed in my new outfit for the evening and done a quick once over in the mirror I sat on my bed realizing I'd overestimated the amount of time it would take me to get ready. I still had over twenty minutes to wait.

I decided to try and read again, but after only a few pages I found myself unable to concentrate, wondering how tonight was going to play out. When I couldn't sit there any longer, I stood up and began straightening the bed, the desk, my nightstand. Before long, I was downstairs straightening pictures and dusting. I heard a light knock on the front door. My heart sputtered then beat furiously. I took a deep breath, attempting to calm myself, as I walked over to the door.

Any illusions that I'd dreamed in the past couple of days were nothing compared to the person standing in front of me. Morgan's dark hair fell loosely over his forehead, slightly disheveled. His deep ocean blue eyes narrowed slightly as the corners of his mouth curved up into a hungry smile.

"You look absolutely mouthwatering," he breathed.

I blushed, attempting to hide my face by reaching for my wallet and keys. "Should I take that as a compliment or run screaming?" I asked, finally looking up, smiling warmly. My heart pounded in my chest and the hair on my arms stood on end from the humming static flickering between us.

"Compliment of course. "His eyes flared briefly, his voice rough. "Besides, you wouldn't make it very far."

I shuddered involuntarily. His eyes focused, watching me before he blinked suddenly, shaking his head.

Looking back to me he said, "We have dinner reservations, perhaps we should go before they become unnecessary."

I nodded, stepping through the threshold and closing the door behind me to lock it. His eyes followed my movement, holding out his elbow as I turned. I slid my hand through as we walked down the steps quietly. Everything seemed smaller now that I was in his company. I felt calm, the energy from him washing over me in cool waves.

Once we were in the car and driving down the road the silence unnerved me. "Why didn't you come looking for me?" I suddenly blurted out.

He smiled warmly, turning his face to my questioning eyes. "I thought you may have needed time to adjust, to be away from all the supernatural things that had been thrust upon you."

"Erin's a mountain lion and my roommate and she was still in my life for the past few days," I pointed out tersely.

"True, but Erin doesn't have the connection we have," he paused, "so she didn't need to take certain precautions before we had dinner tonight."

"Precautions?"

He looked ahead, focusing on the road.

"Yes, I needed to hunt." His voice was subdued, muted.

"People?" I asked softly.

Morgan's eyes narrowed the slightest bit.

"You're inquisitive," he mused, the quiet purr of the engine the only sound in the sleek car. "Perhaps I will explain it to you later."

So, we were back to being evasive, great. I let a few more minutes pass, casually glancing out of the window before I broke the silence again. "So, where are we going?"

His eyes turned playful, "That's a surprise."

I sighed, wondering if I was going to get a straight answer tonight…or ever. "Since you're avoiding all my questions, I have a favor to ask," I said quietly.

His eyebrows raised, eyes focused on the road. "I'm not avoiding, merely stalling remember." He turned to look at me and said, "It's very difficult to share things with someone whose memory I can't erase or alter." He stared into my eyes just long enough for me to want to ask him to watch the road before turning his face forward. "I'd be more than willing to do anything you asked."

I nodded, preparing myself, "I want to find a way to release Chase from the magic binding him to me."

"I'll look into it," he frowned, "but why?"

"Well, I don't think it's fair for him to be tied to me because of some spell, he has a life too."

"That's very considerate and also very difficult. Most magic like that can only be broken when the person who placed it dies. I've seen it happen only once." A hint of sadness formed on his features.

Just my luck, I thought. We rode quietly as I thought about his revelation. Why does everything always have to be so difficult? I wondered. The interstate lights flashed by and faded in the distance as we drove out of the city limits.

"What are your hobbies, other than reading?" His smooth voice rolled over the silence of the car.

"You won't answer any of my questions, but you expect me to tell you about myself."

"I never said I wouldn't answer them, just not yet."

"Same thing."

"Okay, let's make a bargain. I'll answer a question if you'll answer a question. We'll trade back and forth."

I nodded in agreement when he glanced in my direction.

"Hobbies?"

I sighed. "I like being outside, camping, hiking, and such. I guess you could call me an outdoors person."

"Why do you think you like nature so much?"

"Hey now, it's my turn remember." He gestured with his hand to continue.

"What's with the electric current I feel whenever you're around?"

"Pass," he said, a smirk pasted on his face as he stared straight forward.

"That's not fair, I answered yours."

"Pass," he repeated.

I glared out the window momentarily before looking back at him, "Fine. Why don't you tell me something I don't know."

He smiled, "Your heart beats one hundred thousand times in one day, it's impossible to sneeze with your eyes open, and a hamburger at McDonalds cost fifteen cents in 1963, not that I ever ate one."

"Really, well butterflies taste with their feet and the distance between the inside of your elbow and your wrist equals the length of your foot." Ha! He wasn't the only one who knew trivia.

"Frozen milk on a stick is popular in Siberia."

"A tiger's fur is striped and so is its skin."

"The memory of a goldfish lasts three seconds."

"Lettuce that you buy at the store is washed in chlorine."

"Well, I don't buy it. But I am on an unusual diet," he added. I found myself smiling suddenly.

"You're good, really, you are," I paused, "But, I haven't forgotten."

He nodded.

"What were you and Madelyn trying to do to me in the hospital and were you two communicating through thoughts?"

"That's two questions," he argued. I simply clasped my hands together and laid them in my lap, waiting.

He sighed. "We were trying to alter your memory. I was simply trying to confirm something I already knew. But when I wasn't able, she thought she'd give it a try. As for the latter, simply put, yes we can communicate telepathically."

"I thought you had to have eye contact so you could hypnotize them with your eyes while you erased their memory."

He laughed. "You *have* been reading a lot. No, I don't need to have eye contact. It's all in the mind." He was still shaking his head back and forth, smiling.

We had turned down a thin paved drive. Even though it was dark, I could feel the trees pressing themselves close to the car, seemingly reaching out to touch it. The seconds passed by before we reached an opening the size of a few baseball fields. The trees circled the small valley like a wall while the moon's light brightened the roof of a very large two story log cabin. I stared in awe at the beautiful home; every side shined with the opening of a massive window. Only the wrap around porch decorated with a wooden swing and rocking chairs sat shadowed. From the pale light spilling across the yard I could see the many flowers that circled the house. Everything was trimmed and clipped in its proper place. I hadn't realized we'd stopped until he was opening his door to get out and walk around to my side of the car.

As I was getting out, I stated the obvious, "This doesn't really look like a restaurant?"

He smiled, "Observant."

"So, you live here and we're going to have dinner here?" I asked. Was he going to cook? Did vampires cook? The thought of him in a cooking class wearing a pink apron like we'd had to wear when I was in high school made me giggle.

He smiled, "Yes, with Kyle and Mitch. Is this something that amuses you?"

I stifled the laughter that was creeping up my throat, "No, it's just…so you're going to cook dinner for us tonight?"

"That is the plan."

He said this so seriously that I decided to keep the jokes to myself and change the subject. I took the opportunity to try and squeeze in another question, "And Kyle and Mitch are? I remember Madelyn saying something about them."

His lips twitched. "Nice try but no. It's my turn remember," he added, turning my own words on me.

We walked up the wooden steps and into the house. I noticed that he didn't stop to unlock the door.

"I'm sure no one is brave enough to break into this house. That's suggesting that they could even find it," he said as the lights switched on by themselves. I looked around for someone, surprised to see that we were the only ones there.

"Motion censored," he added smiling. Everything was made of rich wood, the walls, the floors, even the various tables that highlighted the room. Everything seemed even bigger than the outside, with high ceilings and wide open rooms. I noticed the far, back wall which held a myriad of large paintings, each one a beautiful landscape. It seemed the room was filled with the same warm colors that were in the pictures. There were a few overgrown chocolate brown leather chairs and one very large matching leather couch in the center of the massive space. To my left was a wide, wooden staircase and to my right stood a huge wooden swinging door. We stood there a moment as my eyes took in the spacious area. This hardly resembled what I'd expected as a home for a vampire.

He placed his hand on the small of my back. I shuddered as I felt the muted hum of energy strengthen. I felt him tense slightly as well.

"I'll show you the kitchen and dining area." He said as he guided me through the heavy wooden door. A kitchen was never mentioned in any of the vampire novels I'd read, but of course there was one since he was planning on cooking. I tried picturing him baking cookies like my dad did from time to time. The thought made me laugh a little.

"Am I missing some hidden vampire joke?"

"No, I just thought it was funny. You know, that you have a kitchen." I suppressed the laugh building in my chest.

"I entertain from time to time," he said mirroring my grin.

The kitchen was almost half the size of the first room we'd been in. It was accented with the same warm earth tones plus a stainless steel refrigerator, oven, and stove. It looked like a kitchen out of one of those home decorating magazines. There was an island in the middle large enough to accommodate a few tall bar stools. On the opposite side of the kitchen was another heavy wooden door.

"What would you like for dinner?" he asked pulling me from my trance.

"Oh, uh. I don't know. So, you actually cook?" I asked still thinking it was a little strange.

"Sure. One has to keep up appearances," he answered steering me toward one of the bar stools. He gently pulled it away from the island waiting for me to sit. I watched as he walked to the other side of the counter slowly rolling up the sleeves of his button up shirt, his dark eyes never leaving mine.

"Do you like steak?" he asked.

"Sounds good to me." The last time I had steak it was in a tiny cardboard container that only took about three minutes to heat in the microwave. A vampire cooking me steak, a little ironic if you ask me.

Morgan opened one door of the large refrigerator and began pulling out vegetables. I looked around the kitchen for a few moments before glancing down at the small bouquet of sunflowers sitting on the counter in front of me.

"I love sunflowers," I said as I leaned forward to smell them.

Morgan paused from cutting the peppers to look at me. He smiled suddenly. "Really? Why?"

"I don't know I love the colors, the yellow and brown and because it's a wildflower, something that grows on its own, untouched and unchanged by human beings. You know they're the only flower that follows the sun. They always face it from dawn until dark. That's pretty impressive if you ask me."

I'd begun to play with the soft petals but now I looked up to see him quietly watching me. His features highlighted with amusement.

"What?" I asked.

"Sunflowers. That must be your flower then. It's a good flower, I guess. Strong. It has a good base."

"My flower, what do you mean *my* flower?"

Morgan had set the peppers aside and was now sautéing a clove of garlic and butter in a skillet.

"I mean that flower is yours. It will heal you when you're hurt, make you happy when you're sad, things of that nature." He paused to place the steak in the pan. "If you eat them when you're healthy they have a sort of alcoholic affect for your kind though."

"Eat them. You're kidding right?"

I watched as he shuffled the pan back and forth. The kitchen was quickly filling with the aroma of garlic. My stomach rumbled loudly.

"No, I'm serious. Try one of the petals." He looked over his shoulder briefly, smiling again.

I sat there for a second wondering if this was a game. He'd probably get a good laugh out of this one. Finally, I sighed and reached over to carefully pull off one of the silky petals from the bunch. From the corner of my view I could see Morgan steeling glances in my direction. I slowly opened my mouth and placed the petal on my tongue. Strangely, it melted instantly. For a moment I felt like a complete idiot. I can't believe I just put a flower petal in my mouth. Seriously, eating flowers? I was about to ask Morgan how funny he thought this was when I started feeling strange. It started in my toes and flowed up my legs to my stomach and arms before it finally hit my head. It was like a liquid fire, but it was ice too. My body felt relaxed, but energized. I felt giddy, like I could do anything.

I giggled and quickly covered my mouth. Where did that come from? My eyes wandered over to Morgan who was placing a plate full of steaming vegetables, perfectly cooked steak, and a slice of ciabatta bread in front of me. There was silverware and a glass of milk there also.

"How did you do that so fast?" I asked bewildered.

He chuckled, "It's the sunflower. You loose track of time. You've been sitting here for a while in a daze. He pulled out the bar stool next to me and sat down. I picked up the fork and cut the tender meat.

"Wow, I think this is the best steak I've ever had. Where did you learn to cook?" I'd never tasted flavors so strongly; the garlic was better than any garlic but not overpowering.

"Various places," he said nonchalantly.

I picked up the glass of milk and drank deeply. Morgan's eyes followed my movements.

"Why do you think you like being outside?" He asked, catching my attention.

"I don't know, I just feel better, like I can think clearer. The air seems fresher, and I love all the sounds." I skewered a few of the vegetables and popped them into my mouth. If the steak was perfect, there was nothing to describe the flavors that came from the vegetable medley. "Who are Kyle and Mitch?" I asked offhandedly.

"You do have a good memory." he commented, still watching me.

"I thought you weren't going to avoid my questions anymore."

He looked down at the table. "They're like me." He paused, gazing up at me from under his lashes and added, "They are good friends of mine that I stay with when I'm in town."

"Favorite music?" he asked next.

"Wait, so where are they now?" I was having a little trouble keeping up with the conversation because my head seemed to be floating in a wonderful fog.

"They went out for the evening."

"You kicked them out so we could have dinner. That's not cool." I said in between a hiccup.

He laughed, "You'll meet them eventually and I didn't kick them out. They had things to do."

"Favorite music?" he asked again.

"Anything and everything, but I tend to favor rock. Why were you in the library that night? No one goes to that floor."

"I told you, you smell different."

"So, you were following me?" I said with another hiccup.

"It's my turn," he reminded me.

I waited, watching as he shifted his eyes to look at the vase of sunflowers. Rather than ask me a question as we had agreed he said, "Yes. At first I thought I just wanted to see who you were, if you were, what you were." He looked back to me, his eyes intense. "But, when you looked up and I saw your face and your beautiful eyes, I knew I wanted to see you again, to hear your voice, to see a smile on your lips."

My cheeks grew hot as I looked away toward my half eaten plate of food, tucking my hair behind my ear. I blinked a few times trying to keep my head from floating off any farther than it had.

"Why do you do that when you're nervous?"

I glanced back at him, "Habit I guess."

He smiled. "You have nothing to be nervous about," he paused, "besides the fact that I am very dangerous and not the best company for you."

"I don't think you'd hurt me."

He frowned. "What makes you believe that?"

"You saved my life, why would you kill me?"

He scowled. "My saving you doesn't negate the fact that I still crave your blood." He hesitated, before continuing, his voice low. "But, I don't think it's that I wouldn't, more so that I can't now. There is something about you that I am drawn to. When you're not around I hunger for it, for you. Not just your blood, but your company. I've been around elves before, but I've never felt this."

I sat there a moment in my daze. "So, the electric current, you feel it as much as I do?"

He nodded as I drank another gulp of milk. From the set of his jaw I could see he wasn't going to say anything else on the topic, so I moved on to my next question.

I felt brave with the icy fire under my skin which is probably what prompted my next stupid question. "You'd mentioned hunting…people?"

His lips twitched as his face shifted, his jaw tightening. I waited patiently, playing with the vegetables with my fork. I watched as his eyes turned to me, conflict raging in them. Time seemed to tick by at an alarmingly slow rate.

Finally, Morgan said, "Yes." His eyes flashed to my face, as I fought to keep my expression even, my emotions calm through the haze. He saw right through me, his lips moving into a crooked smile. "By code, we aren't supposed to kill, just take what we need and alter their memory so it will seem to them like a hazy dream or nothing at all. It is very difficult though, to stop. Sometimes, it is impossible. I try and save those times for the murderers and serial killers, the wicked humans in this world."

I nodded weakly, taking everything in. "What about bite marks?" I questioned.

"Our saliva has a healing agent that makes them seal and disappear in a matter of a few minutes."

I nodded again, sorting through to my next question. He watched me warily, gauging my reactions. "I'm not going to share what you've told me with anyone, if that's what you're worried about," I added briskly.

"It's not that." He leaned forward slightly, "How do you take all of this so coolly?"

I could smell his skin and the clean fabric of his shirt. It was intoxicating. I shook my head trying to stay at least somewhat focused.

"What do you expect me to do, run screaming?"

"Hopefully not. That would not be a healthy decision on your part," he hesitated, eyes searching my face, "but in a way, yes."

"I don't know, I guess, maybe because a part of me always felt like something was out of place in my life. That and the fact that I've also begun to crave the odd humming and your presence when we are not together. For once everything is beginning to fit properly, like a puzzle I've been trying to figure out my entire life." My eyes searched his face as the seconds stretched silently.

"It was difficult...not seeing you the past few days," he said, his voice rough.

"More than you can imagine," I added subdued. He looked down at my plate of food.

"Eat," he murmured.

"Does it taste the same? Food, I mean," I asked, taking a bite of the bread. I tried not to crunch too loudly as I chewed.

He smiled, "It did at first, but as the years passed the taste diminished," he paused, "or perhaps my taste buds lost their memory." I watched as he slowly picked up my fork, skewered a zucchini slice, carefully placed it in my mouth, and chewed, all the while regarding me with a mischievous smile.

"What about light, I know you can go out in it, but why do vampires avoid it?"

"Our skin is so pale that it's more noticeable in sunlight. We try and stay out of people's attention, more like shadows."

"Coffins?"

He laughed. "Myth, I think the same person who came up with that, decided that we originated from Transylvania too, which is completely false. I don't sleep much though, only a few hours every couple of nights because my body doesn't require as much."

"Where are you from?"

"England actually."

"England? What brought you here?"

He took a deep breath, blowing it out slowly as he ran his fingers through his dark satin hair. "I was born and grew up there. My mother and father were common people. We had a small farm, which I worked with my father everyday. I spent most of my evenings lying in the fields gazing at the stars. That was where she found me." He paused, editing, "She was lonely, which is expected of a life like this. We spent a few years hunting together before I branched off on my own. I've traveled the world ever since." His eyes narrowed slightly. "It's difficult sometimes because we can't stay in one place for very long. Once humans begin to notice that you look the same ten years later, it's time for a new place." He looked down at the floor.

"It must be hard." He looked up from beneath his lashes. "Having to move all the time," I added.

He shrugged. "The hard part is when all the people you know from your life pass away, when you are completely alone in a world that doesn't know who you are or that you even exist."

I wanted to hug him, to console him in some way. I slowly reached over to touch his cold hand. He stiffened momentarily, the humming vibration between us increasing, before he took a deep breath, his eyes gazing into mine.

"I'm not safe for you, for your kind" he said flatly, his tone serious.

"Let me be the judge of that."

He raised an eyebrow as his voice turned icy, "I could drain you right here without anyone the wiser. No one would even know you were missing once I erased the memory of those necessary."

I froze, my eyes widening with shock at his words. I was suddenly pulled from my flower petal stupor.

He shook his head, his face ridden with chagrin. "I'm sorry. I just don't think you understand how dangerous I am to you." He moved his hand from under mine, placing it on top. "I'm on my best behavior from now on, scouts honor."

I smiled weakly.

"Any more imaginative questions?" he asked, his lips hinting at a smile.

I focused trying to remember anything else I'd read about vampires in my books. "So garlic isn't a problem but what about crosses and staking?"

"Myth, and definitely myth. We're very difficult to kill. A stake to the heart won't really do anything, although it is extremely uncomfortable for a few days after. I have a heart beat, but it only beats once every few minutes." His voice faded as he looked away.

"So technically you are alive...sort of."

"It depends on how you look at. We're all here by some spark of magic. Mine is just different from yours." He had a point.

"What about your teeth, aren't you supposed to have long fangs?"

He looked back at me, chuckling lightly. "No, no they're there, but you'd never notice them. They grow maybe a millimeter, if that, when I am hungry or in a particularly tense situation, but nothing you could really see without getting really close, which is not something people tend to do knowingly." He added seriously, "Humans tend to avoid of us because of their instincts. I am a predator, you must never forget that."

I sat there remembering the first few times I'd seen him, how I'd wanted to run away from him.

"Can you fly or turn into a bat?"

He set the fork down. "No, I can't do either. I am incredibly strong though and fast, very fast," he finished, his voice low and quiet. "Perhaps I'll show you one day."

I took another bite of bread, chewing carefully as I thought about my next question.

He interrupted my thought process, "What's your favorite card game?"

"Solitaire. Yours?"

"Rook."

I could feel the effects of the flower wearing off but I wasn't ready to loose that feeling yet. I reached over toward the vase to pull off another petal only to find that I was suddenly grasping at air. I looked at Morgan who was still sitting the same as he had been a few moments before. My eyes scanned the room for the vase.

"When did you do that? Did I space out again?"

He was smiling "No, no spacing. I told you, very, very fast."

"That's not possible. I understand fast, but that's not possible. Where are the sunflowers?"

"They're away for now. I can't have an intoxicated elf on my hands. Your type can be a challenge to handle when you get a hold of your flower."

"Aw, is the little half-elf too much for the big bad vampire." I said mockingly. "I just wanted one more."

"Uh-huh. That's how it always starts. It almost always finishes with an elf who's lost her sense of reason for a few days, sometimes weeks." He paused to brush my hair behind my ear. "So, where were we?"

I decided to give up on the flowers seeing that his mind was already set. "So, how were the seventies? I imagine the eighties were pretty fun too."

He laughed and nodded.

The rest of our dinner continued on in the same fashion. When I wasn't asking him about off the wall vampire myths, he was asking me the most ordinary of questions.

I'd forgotten about the time until we were walking out of the front door to the car.

"Are you going to leave the lights on?" I asked as he opened my door.

"Motion censored remember? And Kyle and Mitch are on their way home."

I wonder how he knew they were coming home. I was still feeling a little fuzzy, but I didn't remember seeing him make or receive a phone call.

"Telepathy, remember?" he said tapping the side of his head. I nodded feeling like an idiot.

Once we'd left and were driving down the road in silence I wanted to feel his cool hand close to mine again. I sat there for a few moments, arguing with myself before I reached over and slid mine next to his. My eyes darted between the road and his face, gauging his reaction. I barely saw his jaw clench as I felt the energy coming from him intensify slightly.

We rode a few more minutes before I felt his cold fingers slowly, carefully lace through mine, his eyes never leaving the road. My stomach tightened as butterflies fluttered wildly. I thought I saw his lips twitch, fighting a smile from the corner of my eye. No doubt he probably heard my heart beating furiously inside my chest.

When we slowed to a stop in front of my house I felt my mood drop. I was hoping the ride would've taken longer. I wasn't ready for the night to be over. He turned off the ignition before turning his perfect face toward me. He slowly untangled his fingers, his eyes locked on mine. While he opened his door and walked around to my side of the car, I quickly unhooked my seatbelt. He opened my door, weaving his fingers back through mine as I stepped out. The tingling sensation tickled all the way up my arm.

We quietly walked the short brick path, up the steps, and finally to the front door.

"Thank you," I murmured.

"It was my pleasure," he replied, his smooth voice echoing in the quiet evening. I stood there, looking into his warm eyes as he gazed back. He lifted his hand and carefully brushed his fingers along my cheek, lingering on my throat before he finally rested his hand on my shoulder. He paused, his eyes searching mine, gauging my reaction before his other hand reached over and wrapped around my waist. The humming static between us began to crackle as he slowly leaned forward to place his soft, cool lips against mine.

My blood began to boil as fire ran through my veins. I let out a sigh, my lips parting. My hands reached up and I tangled my fingers in his silky hair as I desperately tried to pull him closer. I felt his body tighten, as his soft lips lifted away from mine, his lashes moving furiously as he blinked. I was using all of my strength, but it wasn't even noticeable as his fingers curled around my wrists, gently loosening my hold on his hair. His clear blue eyes flashed to mine as he kissed the tops of my fingers.

"My self control is far from perfect and you smell absolutely wonderful." His voice came out quiet and rough.

I sighed, "Would you believe me if I told you that I hadn't been expecting that reaction from myself?"

He smiled as he whispered, "Neither was I."

I could feel my cheeks turning red.

"Can I see you again tomorrow?" he asked.

I nodded, the movement feeling fuzzy. "I'd like that." Maybe Morgan was the same thing as a sunflower for me, only better.

He leaned forward, placing his lips quickly against my throat before pulling back, "Tomorrow then."

Chapter 7: Slate Gray

❦

I closed the door behind me in a daze, my entire body tingling. I slowly climbed the stairs and opened my door and laid my keys and wallet on the desk. I stood there, my lips still cool, replaying the night through my head when my eye caught what looked to be a sheet of notebook paper on my bed. I walked over to pick it up, wondering what Erin was up to now. I felt the daze and the evening's comfort dissolve as I read through her quickly scribbled handwriting.

Ansley,

Had to go to emergency meeting. Something isn't right. I'll be back as soon as I can to explain. Be careful.

Erin

I felt the blood drain from my face as I read through the short note again. Erin never wrote like that unless she was upset. Her sentences were never short and choppy.

Pale light spilled into my room from the hall as I heard soft movement at my back. Thinking she'd come back for something she'd forgotten, I started to turn to ask her what was going on when something hard and blunt hit the back of my head. The room spun into darkness before I even hit the floor.

I woke, my body sprawled out against some hard, cold surface. I felt stiff, like I'd been outside too long, the chilly air sinking into my bones. My eyes fluttered open to darkness as I shivered. I lay there a moment, letting them adjust, when finally I was able to decipher what looked to be leaves. I blinked a few more times recognizing the small branched formation of bushes and finally the large round barrels of trees. Apparently, I was somewhere in the woods. When I lifted my head, pushing up with my arms, my head throbbed, making me wince. I brushed off the leaves that were sticking to my face, still feeling completely disoriented as I held my head in my hand trying to ease the hammer that was pounding inside of it.

"She's awake," a gruff voice said. I turned to see two big, younger looking men, both casually leaning against separate trees with their arms folded across their chests, both staring at me. They looked like two guys from the college weightlifting team, one in khakis and a red and white striped polo shirt, the other in blue jeans and a thin black sleeveless muscle-t. I shivered again, cold from the ground and the cool air. I tried to work out in my mind how long I'd been out here. It was still dark so I guessed maybe a few hours.

I looked around for anything familiar, any clues that would tell me if I had any hope at all of finding my way out.

My legs had begun to cramp; I needed to move. I slowly slid my feet under me preparing to stand. The shorter one wearing the black shirt immediately pushed off the tree, stomping toward me, his face twisted with anger. I shrunk back, waiting for his attack.

"Let her stand," said a smooth voice off in the darkness. The one who'd been heading for me stopped and turned around to march back to his perch. I finished standing, my eyes searching the pitch black for where the voice had come from.

They focused on a figure that appeared from behind the trees the two men were leaning against. He walked slowly, his head down. When he was within a few yards he carefully looked up, his eyes dark and a smirk spread across his smooth face.

"Scott?" I gasped in shock.

"Surprising, isn't it?" His voice was calm and level as he took a few steps toward me. He was wearing a slate gray shirt and dark jeans. His eyes shimmered the same color as his shirt, slightly larger and rounded.

He sighed. "But life always seems to be full of surprises."

I stood there quietly as my heart pounded in my chest, watching as he casually paced, each zigzag bringing him a little closer to me. I forced myself to stay as still as possible.

"You're so quiet Ansley. Aren't you going to plead, tell me that someone will be looking for you?"

"No." I could feel a small part of myself burn with anger knowing that he was someone I'd thought I knew, someone who'd betrayed my best friend.

"Probably better, begging annoys me and even if someone were looking for you, they wouldn't make it in time anyway." He became still as he called over his shoulder, "I'll handle it from here. You can head back." The two men smoothly turned and disappeared into the darkness, I shifted my eyes back to him when I could no longer see them.

"I've heard that your blood is some of the sweetest ever tasted." He slinked forward another step.

"H-how am I different from anyone else?" I stalled trying to keep my voice calm, as I trembled, my entire body screaming for me to run.

"Don't play games with me Ansley, you know that your mother was an elf," he warned, his voice low as he took another step. I felt like I was being hunted, a helpless mouse in front of a lethal snake right before it strikes.

"They say half elfin blood is the richest, something about the mixing of human with fey." I watched as a ripple rocked through his body, his movements becoming fuzzy. Knowing what he was about to turn into, I couldn't stop myself as I turned to run. I pushed my stiff legs as fast as they would go not daring to look back. I heard a distinct growling noise that was growing louder, closer.

The sounds behind me faded as I struggled to run even faster when something smacked into my back, sending me to the ground. I rolled to see a wolf duck into the darkness, a vibrating blur, before Scott returned, faster than my eyes could follow.

He stomped over to me as I tried to push myself backwards to stand. He reached down, picking me up by my arms like I was a rag doll and tossing me into a tree. My head collided first, my back second. I slid and slumped down to the ground, everything spinning.

"Why do they always run?" he asked rhetorically as he gracefully weaved in and out of the trees, disappearing and re-emerging from the darkness.

"You know, I wasn't completely positive you were who I was looking for. I mean you had the beautiful green eyes just like your mother. But all my efforts were confirmed when just the other day when, out of the blue, it started pouring rain on a day without a cloud in the sky that I was sure you were the one. Only you have the power to do that. I would've had you if that stupid boy hadn't found you first." He paused as he continued to ease closer.

I remembered seeing the wolf that didn't really look like a wolf. How he'd seemed to understand what I was saying and shuddered from the memory. Had it been raining because I was sad?

"I thought you were a mountain lion?" I asked confused, my head fuzzy.

He chuckled. "So does Erin, but no. I'm much more refined. I can change into anything I want. I've been switching between a mountain lion so I could find out what Erin's pack knows about this area, they're quite powerful you know, and a werewolf so that I would be put in charge of finding and destroying you. Those mutts won't trust anybody but their own kind apparently; but they are determined to rid the world of your kind."

He started speaking again, his voice low and even, "Your mother was very powerful too. So powerful in fact that she could control nature in ways that are unimaginable...just like you." He was still creeping toward me. "That's why she had to die. All of you elves are too influential, there is too much you can control." He paused and eased forward. "Pity that your human father happened to be on the plane with her when it 'mysteriously' crashed." His voice was thick with sarcasm as he chuckled lightly.

As stupid as it was, my mind was screaming at me to try and run again. I slowly pushed myself up, focusing on keeping the ground in place. His eyes flickered over to me, narrowing as he watched me move.

"Go ahead, run, it'll heat your blood up even warmer." He smirked. "I'll even give you a head start."

Before he even finished I took off again, my eyes looking for anything that could possibly save me. I heard the same snarling noises behind me, growing louder as he closed the gap between us when I tripped over a root. My leg twisted as I slammed into the ground. I cried out in pain, my voice echoing in the quiet night air. Tears streamed down my face as I turned to see his shadow in the distance.

I felt time suddenly slow as I thought about what he'd said about my mother, her powers, and I prayed that I had some of the same gift. I looked up to the trees, focusing. I concentrated, thinking about what it would feel like to have a gush of wind sweep through everything, sending him flying into a tree. The air around me started to swirl, lifting my hair and the trees began to rustle when I suddenly felt a sharp pain. The wolf had sunk his teeth into my arm, biting down.

The wind stopped as I screamed in pain. He let go, taking a few steps back before streaming into a hazy blur. Moments later, Scott stood there wearing the same jeans and shirt. I felt my arm growing warm where he'd bitten me as the blood soaked through my shirt.

"Do you think I'm stupid, that I'd let you control these woods?" He stalked toward me. "You're just like the rest of them."

I looked down in those few brief moments before he was on me again. My arm was dripping blood everywhere, the sleeve of my sweater stained darker as it began to saturate my jeans. I clamped my hand down on it, trying to slow the bleeding.

He reached down and yanked me up by the arm he'd bitten while I gritted my teeth in pain. "I thought it was going to be difficult, getting to you. But, Erin was so easy; it was all just a simple illusion," he purred as he held me there. "If Seth hadn't slipped up and killed that student mistaking her for you, and if your stupid vampire hadn't killed Will when he'd almost finished you, this could've been over by now." He smirked. "It would've been an easier death, but now I think your vampire needs to be sent a message."

I pretended to listen to him as I used the opportunity to try and focus again on the trees around me, not knowing exactly what I was able to do. The air had just started sweeping past us again when he threw me into another tree. My good arm hit first. I heard a loud pop and felt something snap. My side hit next and then I landed in a heap. My ribs ached painfully as I writhed on the ground. The air coming in and out of my chest scared me as I wheezed, the noise sounding wet.

"You don't learn do you?" he growled.

I tried to push myself up, glimpsing my bitten arm out of the corner of my eye. My sleeve had been ripped so I could see the bloody marks. The dark liquid flowed faster than seemed possible. My stomach turned, nauseated as I tried to breathe deeply, but I couldn't because of the tight ache in my ribs. *There shouldn't be that much blood,* a panicky voice announced in my head.

I began pulling myself away from the tree, struggling to get my feet under me so I could stand. I was supporting myself on my unbroken arm and knees when I felt his foot connect with my stomach, knocking the air out of me and sending me flying. I threw my arms out, attempting to catch my fall, but it was pointless. My body slammed into the hard ground again. I laid there limp, unable to move as my breathing became even shallower.

My vision was hazy as I watched the same transformation that had happened a few minutes ago. Long fur poked through where his clothes seemed to be quickly dissolving. He crouched in his wolf form in front of me preparing to launch himself on me. I never pictured this as being the way I would die. The heroes in my stories never took their last breath alone in the darkness. Why couldn't something follow along with the books for once? I closed my eyes, bracing myself for the final blow.

"Stop." I heard Morgan's smooth voice growl. My eyes flashed open to the wolf's face inches from my throat. He turned his head, a deep rumble coming from his chest.

I tried to move my arms to push myself back away from him, but they were too heavy. My body felt like a solid numb, heavy weight. Suddenly, he was shifting again. This time I could hear the crunching noises of what sounded like bones breaking and grinding against each other. I closed my eyes for a second and reopened them to see him standing in the same spot in human form. I concentrated on Morgan, feeling my heart skip at the sight of him. I wanted to tell him that it was probably too late, that breathing was becoming too difficult, but my tingling lips wouldn't form the words.

"You think you can stop me vampire?" Scott asked, his voice dark and menacing. "We will destroy their entire society, elves, fairies, and anything else that stands in our way."

He moved quicker than my eyes could follow, a vibration in the air and then his arms were around me, my back to him as he cradled me roughly against him. The quick movement surprised me. I yelled out in pain, everything swirling around me. I felt the arm that had hit the tree sway lifelessly next to me. He was bigger than he looked and hot, the warmth radiating from him almost burned. I could see Morgan standing in the clearing, his face a mask of fury as he took a step forward.

I gasped as Scott tightened his grip on me, "I *will* break her neck. Not that it matters because I'm going to kill her eventually anyway." I fought to keep my eyes open as they continued to grow heavy. I could feel his hot breath on my neck, my hair being pushed aside.

"She does taste good though vampire. I'm surprised you haven't tried her yourself." I felt something warm, moist and soft against my neck. His lips? I shuddered inwardly, every impulse in me wanting to run, kick and fight, anything to get away from him.

Even in the darkness I could see Morgan's face grow paler. His piercing eyes narrowed, a low rumble coming from deep inside him somewhere.

My eyes closed as I began to lose the battle of consciousness, my body feeling like a hollow shell while

I started to drift. Suddenly, the rough arms that had been holding me disappeared and I could feel the weightlessness of falling. I kept waiting for the cold, hard ground to be the final punch. My arms, sapped of energy, wouldn't move to reach out and catch me. But it never came. Instead I was floating, folded into a cool set of arms.

I heard a roar as what sounded like Scott yelled in pain followed by a snarl, and finally silence. The last thing I thought I heard was someone's deep voice say, "Well, that was easier than we'd thought." Then I slipped into the warm pool of darkness.

I knew I was dead but I could hear Morgan's anxious voice calling my name, "Ansley? Can you hear me? Please open your eyes." I felt movement next to me. "Mitch, I've got to get Madelyn. Let me know if anything happens." If anything happens. What was supposed to happen besides my inevitable demise? I was just about to tell Morgan not to bother Madelyn when I fell into pitch black.

I woke again to Madelyn's sweet voice somewhere close by. "She's lost a lot of blood and her breathing is very weak. She won't make it to a hospital."

Cool lips touched my forehead. "Ansley, I need you to open your eyes," Morgan begged, his voice thick.

I wanted to, I concentrated as hard as I could, but couldn't make them budge. I felt cool fingers probing along my arms increasing the pain as I fought to move my eyelids.

"One arm is broken and I think the wound on the other is worsening." Madelyn paused, "Is that what I think it is? Of course, he's bitten her."

Morgan's chest rumbled next to me in a growl before I finally lifted the heavy curtain of blackness.

Forcing my eyes half open as I surfaced from the thick, dark hole.

"Ansley," he said, his voice tight. I struggled to focus, finding that I was still surrounded by darkness, my body quickly making itself known that it was in serious pain. I felt a sharp poking in my side. I gritted my teeth as I felt my eyelids shutting again.

"A few ribs are broken too, I think." Madelyn paused, still feeling, her fingers now examining my head. "A good bump on her head too," she said methodically, looking at Morgan.

"Ansley, everything is going to be fine," I heard Morgan's anxious voice say by my ear.

"I don't think so," I whispered, not knowing if he heard me.

"You can heal her Morgan."

"Yes, but I've seen you use your powers before Madelyn. That's why I brought you here. I need you to fix her. Please." His voice was strained.

"There's too much damage. I wouldn't be able to hold my concentration long enough to do any good. She would most likely end up dying. I'm sorry Morgan. You have to heal her if she's going to live."

I pushed my eyes open, focusing on him. I wasn't too sure I was going to be all for this *healing* process. "Heal me how?" I mumbled.

His jaw tightened as he looked at Madelyn over me. A mix of emotions crossed his face. He looked down, his piercing eyes searching mine. He took a deep breath while his conflicted eyes narrowed.

"I love you," he whispered before I felt a pair of hands lock on my shoulders and another press down on my legs. Where'd that third person come from? I tried to lift my head to look, but couldn't. My heart raced as my breathing became erratic.

"Morgan?" My eyes shifted back to him as he tightened his hands around my arm and leaned his head down, placing his cool lips to the bloody wound.

I screamed in pain, fought against the iron hands that held me as my arm ached. It felt like everything in my arm was squeezing together, like my bones were going to break from the pressure.

"Stop!" I thrashed wildly, putting whatever strength I could into getting free. The constricting weight only worsened. I squeezed my eyes shut, gritting my teeth.

I wanted to sink back into the black hole, wanted it to all go away, when finally the pain began to dull. I took in a ragged breath as my muscles started to relax. I felt something soft against my lips.

"Open your mouth," he said gently. I let it fall open with what little strength I had and felt a cool liquid slowly flow down my throat. The taste was unbelievable. I tried to grab his wrist and realized I was still being held down. I fought against the strong hands that kept me from moving. Slowly, as I felt myself being pulled under I let my body relax.

"I'm dying." I concentrated on forming the words, hoping they were coherent.

"Of course not." I thought I heard amusement in his voice.

Then Madelyn whispered, "We still need to get her to a hospital though."

"Morgan," I muttered and felt his cool fingers trace along my cheek.

"Yes love?"

I remembered that something was still gripping my bottom half. "What's holding my legs?" I mumbled, not sure they heard me.

"Hey, I'm Mitch," a happy, deep voice announced, "Nice to meet ya."

"You too," I murmured before falling into the darkness for the last time that night.

Chapter 8:
Fender Bender

&

I laid there listening to a continuous annoying beep as it grew louder while I drifted up from the hazy cloud of sleep into consciousness. I blinked my eyes to stare up at a high arched ceiling. I shifted, uncomfortable under the soft sheets. I felt like I hadn't moved in days as I maneuvered my heavy arms preparing to push myself up.

"I don't think so." Cool, firm hands pressed down on my shoulders. I looked over to see him sitting next to the bed as he repositioned, resting his arms beside me on the fluffy mattress.

"Morgan." I gasped as I struggled to push myself up again, attempting to reach over and wrap my arms around him, the beeping noise in the background suddenly accelerating.

"Calm down," he whispered, softly placing his hand on my shoulder, his eyes anxious as I winced in pain from my sudden burst of movement. I laid my head against the flat pillow, taking a deep breath.

"Are you okay?" his eyes uneasy as they scanned my face for any sign of discomfort.

I nodded. "I'm so glad you're here." I paused looking around at what looked to be a very large bedroom. "Wait, where is here?"

He smiled. "My bedroom. At least we know your memory is still intact."

I scowled. "Why wouldn't it be? Did you try to mess with my head while I was out? And why am I not in a hospital?"

He chuckled, leaning closer on the bed, his dark hair shadowing his forehead. "No, but you did have a nasty bump on it," he paused, averting his eyes to look at the tubes weaving up my arms, "I thought about it though. Maybe then you could have a normal life again." His voice was subdued as his expression became solemn.

"I like the life I have now," I said, panic squeezing my throat.

His eyes shifted back to mine, somber.

I scrambled for something to say, "And besides, we both know it wouldn't have worked. So, what happened?"

"A lot." He frowned, contemplating. "Where should I begin?"

"How about with why I'm here instead of a hospital and how you have all these machines hooked up to me? Did you steal them?"

He laughed, "No, I didn't steal them. Madelyn borrowed them." He paused. "You're here because it is much easier to heal you here instead of a hospital. Try explaining to someone why you're putting sunflowers in a saline bag instead of saline."

I looked at the clear plastic bag hanging from the metal stand, confused because it wasn't full of bright yellow sunflower petals.

"It's the liquid from the sunflowers. Each petal is pressed in a machine. Let's just say it takes a lot of sunflowers to fill that bag."

"Why couldn't I just eat them like you said?"

"Your injuries were too extensive," he said gloomily.

"How did you know where to find me?"

"That wasn't so difficult. I'd just started hunting with Kyle and Mitch when Erin called me once she'd gotten back to the house. She said she smelled a wolf and had a bad feeling because the door was unlocked and lights were on, which is apparently something you never do."

I nodded, mentally confirming the fact that she knew me too well. He leaned a little closer so that his smooth face was just inches from mine. When he spoke again his voice was muted as the words raced out of his mouth, almost too fast for me to hear.

"I panicked at first, afraid that you were in danger, that something had happened to you. Erin waited for me so we could all search. We followed their scent for a few miles, but it split up once we got into the woods. She called on her pack and we went our separate ways, following the two different paths."

I interrupted, "I remember Mitch at first but not Kyle and didn't you leave or something? I thought I heard you tell Mitch to let you know if anything happened, which I thought was funny because I wanted to tell you I really didn't think I had much hope of making it…" My voice trailed off as I watched him quietly smiling at me. "What?" I asked confused.

"You're rambling."

I nodded and laughed a little. "Yeah, guess I am. Sorry."

"I don't mind. I like it." He paused before continuing, "Yes, I did leave to get Madelyn. It was quite funny actually. When I showed up in her living room her reaction was priceless. I don't think she liked traveling that fast though. Nymphs aren't too keen on light speed."

When he'd told me he was fast I didn't even consider that amount of speed and Madelyn a nymph? What else exists out there? I did my best to keep my jaw from dropping.

"Wait, nymph?"

"Yes, she comes from a long line of nymphs who have the power to heal with magic." Whoa. I added that to the list of things I never thought I'd hear.

He smiled at my reaction as he continued, "As for Kyle, he was busy cleaning up the mess."

I nodded, taking a good guess as to what the "mess" was.

"We came across two of them, the one wearing the black shirt ducked and ran before we even had a chance, but the other one stayed and fought. It wasn't a problem for the three of us."

I shuddered, remembering them leaning against the trees.

Morgan's anxious eyes flickered to my face, "What hurts? I can go get Madelyn." He leaned away as if he were on the verge of running out the room to get her.

"No, I'm fine, I was just remembering the guys you're talking about."

His face became serious, his lips pressed together as his jaw tightened.

"S'okay, I'm fine. Everything is fine." I laid my hand on his, my fingers tracing little circular patterns over the cool skin. He sighed, relaxing as he leaned forward again to put his face close to mine.

"We continued to follow their trail," he paused, "then I heard him, the things he said, your screams. It took everything I had not to leave the others to finish finding you in the darkness." His face was tense, serious as he continued, "But we couldn't, because he was very smart and would've run, which would've put all our work back to square one. So, we quickly devised a plan that left me as the distraction while they made a wide circle and snuck up behind him. When I saw you lying on the ground, your heartbeat was so faint. Then you opened your eyes to look at me and you looked so scared, so broken. I wanted to break every bone in his body, piece by piece. I almost ruined the plan when he picked you up. I almost destroyed him right then." He ran his hand through his hair, blowing out a breath of air. I quietly watched him, patiently waiting for him to continue.

"I still didn't know if you were going to make it, you were barely breathing and your blood, I could smell your blood all around me." He moved his other hand on top of mine, mimicking the circular patterns that I was tracing on his. I let out a sigh, the feeling of his cool fingers calming me.

"It was difficult...to stop." His searching eyes met mine. "I've never had blood like yours before," he paused, "it was so smooth, pulsing with this sugary taste that made me want it to never end."

"And you gave me yours right?"

He nodded.

"So shouldn't I be a vampire now too?"

He leaned back laughing, a velvety rumble in the quiet room.

"Still believing all that mythological stuff are we?" His laughter slowed as he leaned forward again to gently brush my cheek with his icy fingertips. I shivered, closing my eyes as I subtly leaned my head into his hand.

"No, you're still you, elf and all." I opened my eyes as he slid his hand back to its position on top of mine.

"You see, because of the magic already in your blood, there is a different reaction when another supernatural being's mixes with it. For instance, when a werewolf bites a normal human, unless they kill them, that human becomes a werewolf."

I took a deep breath, glad that I didn't have to worry that I'd be howling at the moon anytime soon.

"You're different. A shifter's saliva carries venom that is poisonous to fey because your blood is so valuable. It makes it so that no matter how small the bite, your blood will flow from the wound faster over time, ultimately killing you."

I interrupted, confused, "Wait, valuable how?"

"Your blood, unlike a normal human's, makes other supernatural creatures stronger, faster, and can even give them a few powers for a short period of time. Your blood for supernaturals is like what a sunflower does for you, only more."

"That's good to know, I guess."

"I had to draw the venom out of your blood before giving you mine. I gave you a very small amount, enough so you could make it here and live."

"Any changes I need to know about?"

"The average human being would've died and changed into my kind. You on the other hand, will benefit with more strength and of course quicker healing abilities for a little while."

He sat there, gauging my reaction, before he continued, "Erin showed up with her pack when we'd begun leaving the woods."

"Scott!" I breathed.

"She knows. She's mad at herself for not figuring it out sooner. That's why they had a meeting, apparently one of the werewolves was discovered and they managed to get the information out of him. She didn't think Scott would act so quickly. She tried to get back as soon as possible to protect you."

"So, they've known about the werewolves trying to kill people like me?"

"You'll have to ask Erin about that one. I can't share any of their secrets. She's here by the way, and so is Chase."

"Chase is normal," I blurted out. Morgan leaned his head to one shoulder, a questioning look on his face.

"I mean if the spell was lifted when my parents were killed in that plane crash a few months ago he's been here because he wants to be, not because of magic." I felt the tears rising as I explained. I took a sharp breath, slowly letting it back out.

"He's a good friend," Morgan finished for me.

I nodded while he brushed my cheek with the back of his hand. "Wait, why is he here?"

"Well, you've been out for a few days and he became worried and started stopping by your house...a lot. I've erased a few things from his memory and added a few things; so long story short is you have nothing to worry about. Just act normal."

"Okay." I said unsure of everything. I barely noticed as a few minutes slipped by in silence. The sunflower saline was definitely working.

"I was wondering if you'd like to spend the day together, say Saturday."

I frowned. "What day is it anyway?"

"Wednesday."

I laid my head against the pillow deflated, "I can't believe I've been out of it for that long."

"You needed to rest, you were..." His voice faded as it trailed off, the muscles in his jaw tensing. I wished I could get up and leave, I was already tired of being cooped up.

"What all was broken?" He was about to speak when Madelyn opened the door and glided in, a warm smile on her smooth, tan face. Her dark curls bounced carelessly around her shoulders as she strode over to the side of the bed, checking the monitor and the clear bags of fluid hanging on the tall metal stand. She didn't look like what I thought nymphs looked like. I thought they were short, angry little creatures; maybe that was dwarves.

"How are you feeling?" her musical voice asked.

"Okay, considering."

Her small fingers began gently lifting my arm to unwrap the layers of spongy gauze.

"You're healing well. The few broken ribs you had have mended almost completely and your arm should be healed by Friday." She'd finished unwinding the sheer fabric. I looked down at the mangled pink scar that shouldn't have looked so good in such a short amount of time.

My eyes shifted between them, marveling.

"I told you, it's my blood and the sunflowers. It'll slowly wear off in the next few weeks," Morgan answered.

Madelyn stood there beaming down at me. "Have you told her yet?" she asked. He raised his eyes to the ceiling, before scowling at her.

"Told me what?"

"Thanks a lot Mattie." He groaned.

Her smile widened as she turned to leave. "Glad to see you're feeling better."

"Thank you." I waited until the door clicked shut before I turned to look at him. "Told me what?" I repeated, attempting to be patient.

"You never did answer about Saturday," he asked, his eyes wide with innocence like he hadn't just side stepped my question.

"Nice try," I said through slightly gritted teeth.

He sighed. "You know about the energy between us?"

I nodded.

"Notice how it's gone now?"

I blinked, my mind trying to feel for it.

"We had some sort of connection. Your mother placed a spell so that I could find you. When I took your blood and gave you mine it sort of sealed the deal apparently. You'll notice some changes."

"Wait, you knew my mother? Why didn't you tell me about this, you've been dodging this since we met... you lied to me...and what sort of changes?" I finished in a rush.

"Lied? When have I lied?" he asked innocently.

"Mmm, how about when you said you'd been following me because you wanted to see if I was a threat and who I was. You knew how to find me, you knew who I was and you're still not telling me why you didn't tell me you knew my mother." I sat there with my arms crossed, scowling at him.

"I didn't lie. I merely bent the truth in a way that would make it easier for you to understand in the long run. You wouldn't have listened otherwise. I told you that you were different. As for the changes, I will know where you are now. It becomes hazier the farther we are away from one another, but you'll understand eventually because you'll know where I am as well." He hesitated then added, "If we were to share blood again, the tighter the bond would grow."

"Just saying *you're different* one night in the library while looking at me quizzically and never giving any more of an explanation doesn't really cover the whole basis," I said miffed before adding quietly, "I kind of had a feeling about that, the changes and whatnot. I thought I felt when you came in."

He nodded, and then changed the subject abruptly, as if he were avoiding something.

"So about Saturday?"

"That's Halloween isn't it?"

He nodded.

"Sure. What'd you have in mind?"

Shrugging, "Kyle won't leave me alone about wanting to meet you. He keeps complaining because he had to clean up that shifter while we were taking care of you and we have a meeting here that night. I thought you might want to be here for it."

I raised one eyebrow. "Anything else you needed to tell me?"

"About what?" he asked innocently.

"I don't know, about my powers, about us, anything that you're currently trying to avoid," I hesitated, "about my mother and the fact that you never shared the critical fact that you knew her."

He smirked. "You're right Halloween does tend to be a very active night in our world and I'd like to know that you're safe."

I snorted. "I think I can handle myself better now." I waited as patiently as possible. The suspense was beginning to drive me crazy.

He leaned even closer, so that his cool breath brushed across my face, "There are more dangerous things out there than vampires and werewolves, things more dangerous than what you've read in your books." His voice was grave.

There was a light knock on the door as Chase stuck his smiling face in.

"Chase!" I struggled to push myself up, wincing in my efforts. Morgan suddenly stood, sliding his hands under my arms, gently pulling me up in to a sitting position.

"Thank you."

He nodded, still standing next to me protectively.

"Ansley, I'm so glad you're okay. I've never seen a vehicle look that messed up before," Chase said.

I shifted my eyes over to Morgan, raising an eyebrow. He avoided me by looking at Chase and saying, "I know, I keep telling her she needs to slow down on those curves. She did some pretty good damage to the tree though." I could here the sarcasm in his voice. Chase, of course was clueless.

Chase shook his head in mock disappointment, "You really should listen to him, Ansley. Lucky you were driving his car instead of your jeep. I know you couldn't live without that beast." He looked up at Morgan, "Not that it's any better that your Audi is a junker now. Now, that was a nice car."

I started to scowl up at Morgan when he looked down at me and winked.

"It's just a car, not something that I can't replace." He paused before adding, "I'll leave you two alone. Do you want anything to eat? I think I'll make a sandwich."

I snorted. His lips curved into a crooked smile as he carefully leaned forward to press his cold lips to my forehead. "I'll be back shortly," he said to me. Looking back to Chase he said, "I'm glad you were able to drop by."

"Same here."

Morgan turned swiftly, gliding out of the room. As soon as the door closed Chase sat down on the bed next to me. "Boyfriend huh? How did I not know about this?"

"Who said he was my boyfriend?" I was still miffed about the fact that he'd felt the need to destroy his beautiful car. What had Morgan erased and added to Chase's memory?

"Come on Ansley, he's crazy about you."

"What gave you that idea?"

"We had a little while to get to know each other while you were…err, recovering."

"You what? What did you talk about?"

"Calm down," he patted my shoulder softly, "not much really. He just mentioned that he was going to be in your life now and was happy that you had me all this time. I did most of the talking. He seems like a decent guy. It was lucky his friends were driving by when they were. I guess they helped him pull you out. Surprisingly, he didn't have get a scratch on him. The man's got luck if you ask me. So, how long have you two been dating?"

I shrugged. "Not long, only one real date I think."

He grinned. "You like him more than you're letting on."

Nodding, "I love him," I added quietly.

He patted my shoulder gently and said, "I figured as much. Do I need to give him the *I'll destroy you if you hurt her speech?*"

I let out a small laugh, the idea of Chase giving Morgan *the speech.*

"No, but thanks," I paused, looking at him, "and Chase, thank you for being here, in my life. You're more of a best friend than anyone could ask for."

"I feel the same about you, Ansley." He bent over to lightly place his lips on my forehead. "I'm glad to see you're happy."

The door cracked open again and Erin stepped in. "I heard someone was finally awake," she said, grinning as she strode over to the opposite side of the bed from Chase.

Her lips twitched as she smiled and nodded at Chase when his cell phone started vibrating in his pocket. He pulled it out, rolling his eyes as he glanced at the little plastic screen, "Great, it's Krystal again." He sighed. "I'll be back. You okay Ansley?"

"Yeah."

He patted my shoulder again as he eased off the bed and put the phone to his ear. Erin and I listened to him as he walked out of the room and flashed us a quick smile before shutting the door.

She sat down next to me on the bed. "How are you feeling?"

"Bruised," I murmured before she suddenly wrapped her arms around me.

"I'm so sorry I didn't get back in time to warn you. I feel like such an idiot for not figuring it out sooner."

I winced, trying not to grunt in pain. "No, no. It's okay, it wasn't your fault," I soothed her as I attempted to hug back. I settled for lightly patting her on the back.

She leaned away, her features animated. "Once we got the information out of the one, I rushed to the house as fast as I could but you were gone," she continued to ramble on while I nodded slowly.

"We've discovered there's an entire network of werewolves that have formed to kill your kind. I guess they're now trying to branch out to shifters. My pack is organizing a defense. I'm just praying it doesn't turn into a war." She rolled her eyes with the last sentence then scrunched her face, puckered her lips and asked, "So, you're definitely an elf huh?"

"Half."

She nodded then frowned. "No pointy ears?" She leaned her head to the side, her eyes examining the side of mine. "I forget those take a while to grow. They usually start in your early twenties." My eyes widened with fear, *pointy ears?*

She laughed. "I'm just kidding Ansley." She was still half giggling when she added, "You will be very powerful though. Your mother was well known throughout the community. I'd heard of her but never actually met her. She was definitely someone special."

"Where'd you hear that from?"

"Morgan surprisingly, I think he's kind of warming up to me seeing as how I'm your roommate and best friend and all." It figured he'd distract me from talking about my family, yet again. I wondered what else he was hiding.

"Why don't you guys like each other in the first place?"

She shrugged. "It goes way back, shapeshifters, werewolves, and vampires have never gotten along. I think it's kind of like a 'who's superior' thing."

"Huh." Well there was one thing that followed along with every story I'd ever read.

"I cleaned the house," she said excitedly.

"Really?"

"Yeah, I've missed you and figured it'd be a nice welcome home gift. It definitely sucks not having you there."

The door opened silently as Morgan stepped through. I watched as they both became tense. He stiffly walked over to the side of the bed opposite her. My eyes danced back and forth between them, waiting for one of them to break the silence.

Morgan's lips crooked up into a small smile. "Erin." Her name flowed out smooth and even as he stood there motionless.

She stayed as still as him and said, "Morgan."

Geesh, I wonder how they ever managed the conversation Erin had been telling me about. At this rate it must've taken them a few hours just to form a sentence.

Erin suddenly glanced down at her watch and said, "Oh crap, I've got to get back. We've got another meeting today." She flashed me a quick smile. "Call me if you need anything, k?"

"Sure, thanks for coming to see me."

She laughed. "Of course, wouldn't miss you for the world."

She patted my hand before her gaze flickered to Morgan then she turned to stride out of the room. The same crooked smile played on his flawless lips as he watched her leave.

As soon as the door closed, I looked over to him. "How was your sandwich?"

His eyes shifted to mine as his smile widened. "Plain compared to you."

"What did you do to your car?" I glowered at him as he smoothly walked over to the opposite side of the bed and sat down next to me in one quick motion.

"You should know, you're the one who crashed into a tree, or don't you remember?" he teased.

"Yeah, real funny."

"Kyle and Mitch had a lot of fun fabricating the scene."

"Uh-huh. And what are you supposed to drive?"

"I'll buy another one."

"You didn't have to wreck your car. I just don't understand why you had to destroy it in the first place."

"It was the quickest and easiest excuse. We were in a hurry and besides I couldn't use your vehicle. I've seen how you look at that thing. You love it too much."

I huffed, deciding I wasn't going to win this argument with him. "So, when exactly do I get to go home, see the light of day, be outside and such?"

"Madelyn said she wanted to keep you here until tomorrow, just to make sure everything is okay."

I sighed and nodded. I needed to be outside in the sun or the rain. I didn't care which as long as I could breathe in the fresh air.

"What do you know about my mom?" I said finally.

His eyes narrowed the slightest bit before he shrugged. I could tell something was missing, could feel its emptiness in the space between us.

"What aren't you telling me?"

His head fell slightly as his jaw tightened. He let out a long sigh. "Your mother and I were very good friends." His eyes flickered to mine as he paused, gauging my reaction. I held my face as still as possible as I gazed back into his dark eyes. He finally nodded and continued, "Even though I was years older than her, I think she saw me as more of a son. The first time I met her was at a meeting of the Elite. She had this warmth about her, this life. Our friendship was something that no one ever knew existed. I remember the last meeting I saw her at. It was being held in hopes of creating new ways to take a stand against the ones who are trying to start a war. She confided in me about you. She told me she wanted me to find you, but wouldn't tell me why." He paused again, hesitating a few moments then added, "It was a few days before she boarded the plane..." His voice trailed off as he watched my eyes shift away to look out the window. I took a deep breath, trying to fill the hollow cave in my chest with air.

"She was amazing, full of life and beauty." His fingers touched my chin, gently pulling my face around so that his was inches from mine. "You look just like her," he added, his cool breath tickling my nose. A mix of emotions raced through me as I controlled my breathing, the machine in the background beginning to beep faster.

Morgan was slowly closing the small gap between us when I frowned and asked, "Wait, what's the Elite?"

He mirrored my frown, the lines above his eyes knitting together slightly, "It's a small group of very powerful supernatural beings that was created to uphold the balance between nonhumans." It sounded like a line from an add campaign. The few, the proud, the Elite.

The pieces clicked together in my mind with an almost audible snap. "So, you're part of the Elite," I said as I watched his pale face smooth over.

"Yes," he answered keeping his expression devoid of any emotion.

"Exactly how powerful are you?" I asked quietly.

"Very," he breathed as he inched his face closer to mine once more.

Epilogue: A Meeting

❧

I opened my door to find him standing there casually waiting in faded blue jeans and a gray hooded OSU sweatshirt. His deep blue eyes stood out against his creamy, smooth skin. His flawless lips stretched into that crooked smile I loved. He slowly leaned forward, placing his hands gently on either side of my face before he pressed his cool lips against mine. I leaned into him, wrapping my arms around his waist as my lips parted. My head began to spin as he slowly leaned away, still smiling. His eyes seemed even bluer as they gazed into mine hungrily.

"Hi," I breathed.

He chuckled a quiet, "Hello."

I'd spent the duration of the morning flitting around my room getting ready. I couldn't find anything to wear and ended up settling on jeans and a black sweater. I was just sliding on my boots when I felt him outside the door, even before he'd knocked.

He was definitely right about one thing, we were connected now.

All of my nervousness seemed to dissolve as soon as I'd opened the door to see him smiling.

"Are you ready?" he asked.

"Will I ever be?"

"True," he mused.

I sighed, grabbing my keys and wallet. As we walked down the brick path I focused on his car. I continued heading in its direction when I felt his cool fingers wrap around my arm pulling me to a stop. I looked at him confused.

"How about you drive today," he said. I could see the new shiny, onyx black Audi parked in the driveway out of the corner of my eye.

He was already tugging me in its direction.

"I don't know, I wrecked your last one if I remember correctly," I said.

We stopped beside the driver's side door. He stood there smiling while he pulled out a set of keys from his sweatshirt pocket, pressing one of the little square buttons. We listened as the doors clicked to unlock. He reached past me, opening the door before turning to hold the keys out in front of my face. I sighed as I held my hand out. He dropped them into my waiting fingers before turning to walk around to the other side of the vehicle. I slid into the smooth leather seat, admiring the clean beige color of everything. I looked over to him, as he sat there smiling at me.

"Seatbelt," I grumbled.

"I'm fine, let's worry about you."

I rolled my eyes, clicking mine into place before turning the key. The engine purred quietly. It was completely different from my jeep's loud rumble.

"I know I've been there but I definitely don't remember how to get back." I said finally.

"You're not the only one. There's a spell on the land so that no one can find it once they've left. Only the people who live there and who are written into the spell will be able to find the place."

I'd begun slowly backing out of the driveway.

"Take a left onto the main road and get on Hwy 34 West."

The ride was relatively quiet. I caught myself stealing glances at him.

"Take this exit."

We continued to drive, drifting farther and farther away from the city, the road beginning to wind and curve. Everything was green and mossy, it was beautiful.

"Turn here," he said abruptly. I turned onto a narrow paved road that continued to wind stretching on and on, the trees a canopy above us. I could see a clearing in the distance, an area where sunlight was streaming through in hazy streaks. The house slowly appeared as we got closer.

It was nothing like I would have guessed. I mean everything was the same with the rocking chairs and log cabin part, but the flowers that I'd seen that night were even more beautiful then I could've imagined. They surrounded the house while the sunlight made the grass a shade of green that matched each flower perfectly. I stopped the vehicle in front of it, staring. I could see Morgan gazing at me out of the corner of my eye.

"It's a little different in the daylight isn't it?" he asked amused.

I nodded slowly, still peering up at the huge house. When I finally pulled my eyes away from it and over to him, I saw he was smiling.

Morgan came around to my side of the car and opened my door. "Don't be nervous," he said quietly.

I shifted my eyes from the large house to him. "Who said I was nervous?" I asked as I slid out of the vehicle and looked up into his warm eyes.

He smiled. "You didn't have to *say* anything."

"I'm walking into a houseful of vampires who know that I taste better than most. Sure. That makes me a little edgy."

He shook his head. "You're wrong, you taste the best." He placed his hands on the vehicle on either sides of my shoulders, forcing me to lean my back against it, his face inches from mine. "I could take your mind off of it, if you like." His cool breath tickled my nose as I looked into his dark blue eyes. My heart began to beat faster as I tried to keep my breathing normal. My eyes closed as he slowly leaned forward, his nose softly tracing a line from my chin to the corner of my jaw. I shuddered when I felt his cool breath against my neck, as his soft lips touched my throat lightly.

I clenched my hands in fists at my sides trying to control myself. Inevitably, I gave up and reached up to wrap my hands around his waist attempting to pull him closer. I felt him tense slightly before he leaned back, a smile playing on his perfect lips.

He stood there a moment, his intense eyes slowly calming before he finally breathed, "Better?"

I nodded, dazed and slightly dizzy. His hand slid down my arm, his fingers lacing through mine as we turned to walk toward the large cabin.

The inside seemed even bigger than it had that night. The wood that covered everything seemed even richer and warmer. We stood there a moment; my eyes took in the spacious area before Morgan called out their names in a voice so quiet that only I should've been able to hear.

Madelyn was the first to appear at the top of the stairs, her face warm as she smiled down at us. A dark haired, pale man walked through a doorway I hadn't noticed at the back of the room and a tall blonde, almost boyish looking person stepped through the door to my right, flashing a view of a kitchen. I wondered if the sunflowers were back on the kitchen island again. My mouth watered in anticipation.

Dr. Blake was the last one I noticed as he looked up from reading a book in one of the big leather chairs. Had he been sitting there the whole time?

We all remained motionless a moment, silent, before the dark haired one strode up to me, extending his hand. "I'm Mitch. We've met already."

I mustered up a smile. "So you were the unlucky one who drew the short stick and had to hold the legs of the nearly lifeless, flailing girl."

He laughed. "Hey, she's got a sense of humor," he paused, smiling at me, "and I don't think I drew the short stick, I was rather lucky that evening." He winked at me. A low rumble sounded from Morgan, whose fingers tightened around mine. Mitch shrugged, turning to sit on the arm of one of the leather chairs, still grinning.

Madelyn was at the bottom of the stairs now, walking over to me. I felt Morgan tense next to me as she reached out, wrapping her small arms around me in one smooth movement.

"We're glad you came," she whispered.

I nodded, hugging her back. Morgan leaned his head in the direction of the boy standing in the kitchen doorway.

"That's Kyle."

He raised his hand in a wave and said, "What's up."

Morgan's eyes shifted back forward. "And you remember Reilly."

He smiled warmly, "It's good to see you again Ansley."

"You too Dr. Blake."

He waved his hand in the air. "Please, call me Reilly."

"Reilly."

We stood there for a moment, the silence on edge before Madelyn's sweet voice inquired, "You haven't told her yet have you?"

"No, I figured she was already stressed enough about coming over here and that it would be best if Reilly did, since he knows more than I do." Morgan looked at Madelyn pointedly as she shrugged, gliding away to sit in one of the overgrown leather seats.

"I'm not stressed," I mumbled. Five pairs of eyes focused on me, their expressions all holding different variations of amusement.

"I heard your mother was quite resilient too," Reilly announced as he folded a page in his book and laid it on the sleek wooden end table next to him. I felt my pulse quicken at the mention of her. Morgan took my hand in his, leading me over to the leather couch across from Reilly.

"Why didn't you tell me you knew my mother?" I repeated the same question I'd asked Morgan a few days ago.

"I didn't know her, but I have gathered more information." He paused as his eyes flickered to Morgan before returning to me. "I'm guessing you know that she had powers, that she could control nature and that she was part of a group of people known as the Elite."

I nodded as my eyes flashed to Morgan.

"There's more." He shifted in his chair, leaning forward. "Only a few people knew she had a daughter, a secret she desperately tried to keep in order to protect you and so that you would have a chance of living a normal life." He inhaled deeply before blowing out in one long breath, "There will be others searching for you."

"Why?" I asked.

"You have her blood running through your veins. Technically, you're supposed to take her place. As for the latter, others merely want you eliminated along with the entire fey society.

"Some are afraid of the powers your people carry and want them gone," Morgan added.

I sat there a moment silently letting everything sink in. I could feel all of them watching me, waiting.

"So, what do I do now?" I finally asked.

"That's entirely your decision. You can stay hidden and continue on with your life or you can assume her role. Either way, it would be to your advantage to learn how to use your abilities. I know someone that I can call for help with that, if that's what you decide."

I nodded in a daze. I vaguely heard him excuse himself and barely felt Madelyn's soft hand on my shoulder before they all disappeared.

I felt Morgan's cool fingers gently touch my chin as he turned my face toward him so that his dark blue eyes could stare into mine. "No matter what you decide, everything is going to be okay. I will be here for you as long as you want me to."

"I will always want you," I quickly blurted out. "But it seems that now I could be a danger for *you* to be around."

He smiled. "Not nearly as dangerous as I am to you." He leaned down to gently place his cool lips to my throat.

"Ha, that's only because as a normal guy would, you assume. I can move trees you know…well, maybe someday." I felt his lips form a smile against my skin.

I sunk into silence, frowning at the thought of the decisions I now had to make.

"I love you," I whispered in a rush, "I wanted to tell you that night, I don't know why I didn't."

"You should know that you are the one human being that I have ever loved, the one person I have ever had these feelings for." His eyes left mine and his smile faded a bit. "I don't think I could live in a world without you in it now," he finished, his voice muted.

This time I reached over and gently touched his cold chin with my fingers, turning his face to me.

"You should know that we see things the same."

He nodded as his lips twitched into a smile before he leaned toward me to carefully place them against mine one more time.

5143078R0

Made in the USA
Charleston, SC
05 May 2010